"What do you see?"

"A pretty white flower. That's why I picked it and put it in my hair.

"But it is not a pretty white flower. Not to me, anyhow. Your eyes perceive light with wavelengths between about 4000 and 7200 angstrom units. The eyes of a Vegan look deeper into the ultraviolet, for one thing, down to around 3000. We are blind to what you refer to as "'red,' but in this 'white' flower I see two colors for which there are no words in your language. My body is covered with patterns you cannot see, but they are close enough to those of the others in my family so that another Vegan, familiar with the Shtigogens, could tell my family and province on our first meeting. Some of our paintings look garish to Earth eyes, or even seem to be all of one color—blue, usually—because the subtleties are invisible to them. Much of our music would seem to you to contain big gaps of silence, gaps which are actually filled with melody. Our cities are clean and logically disposed. They catch the light of day and hold it long into the night. They are places of slow movement, pleasant sounds. This means much to me, but I do not know how to describe it to a—human."

He is a cultured man, the ambassador from Vega. Yet he must die, to preserve the sovereignty of Earth—or so Conrad Nikomos has been told. The truth is less simple.

THIS IMMORTAL

To Ben Jason

THIS IMMORTAL

ROGER ZELAZNY

ace books
A Division of Charter Communications Inc.
A GROSSET & DUNLAP COMPANY
51 Madison Avenue
New York, New York 10010

An ACE Book

This Ace printing: September 1980

Published Simultaneously in Canada

8 0 9
Manufactured in the United States of America

"YOU ARE A KALLIKANZAROS," SHE ANNOUNCED SUDDENLY.

I turned onto my left side and smiled through the darkness.

"I left my hooves and my horns at the Office."

"You've heard the story!"

"The name *is* 'Nomikos.'"

I reached for her, found her.

"Are you going to destroy the world this time around?"

I laughed and drew her to me.

"I'll think about it. If that's the way the Earth crumbles—"

"You know that children born here on Christmas are of the kallikanzaroi blood," she said, "and you once told me that your birthday—"

"All right!"

It had struck me that she was only half-joking. Knowing some of the things one occasionally meets in the Old Places, the Hot Places, you can almost believe in myths without extra effort—such as the story of those Pan-like sprites who gather together every spring to spend ten days sawing at the Tree of the World, only to be dispersed at the last moment by the ringing of the Easter bells. (*Ring-a-ding*, the bells, *gnash, gnash,* the teeth, *clackety-clack,* the hooves, et cetera.) Cassandra and I were not in the habit of discussing religion, politics, or Aegean folklore in bed—but, me having been born in these parts, the memories are still somehow alive.

"I am hurt," I said, only half-joking.

"You're hurting *me,* too. . . ."

"Sorry."

I relaxed again.

After a time I explained, "Back when I was a brat, the other brats used to push me around, calling me 'Konstantin Kallikanzaros.' When I got bigger and uglier they stopped doing it. At least, they didn't say it to my face—"

"'Konstantin'? That was your name? I've wondered. . . ."

"It's 'Conrad' now, so forget it."

"But I like it. I'd rather call you 'Konstantin' than 'Conrad'"

"If it makes you happy . . ."

The moon pushed her ravaged face up over the windowsill to mock me. I couldn't reach the moon, or even the window, so I looked away. The night was cold, was damp, was misty as it always is here.

"The Commissioner of Arts, Monuments and Archives for the planet Earth is hardly out to chop down the Tree of the World," I rasped.

"*My* kallikanzaros," she said too quickly, "I did not say that. But there are fewer bells every year, and it is not always desire that matters. I have this feeling that you *will* change things, somehow. Perhaps—"

"You are wrong, Cassandra."

"And I am afraid, and cold—"

And she was lovely in the darkness, so I held her

in my arms to sort of keep her from the foggy foggy dew.

In attempting to reconstruct the affairs of these past six months, I realize now that as we willed walls of passion around our October and the isle of Kos, the Earth had already fallen into the hands of those powers which smash all Octobers. Marshaled from within and without, the forces of final disruption were even then goose-stepping amidst the ruins —faceless, ineluctable, arms upraised. Cort Myshtigo had landed at Port-au-Prince in the antique *Sol-Bus Nine,* which had borne him in from Titan along with a load of shirts and shoes, underwear, socks, assorted wines, medical supplies, and the latest tapes from civilization. A wealthy and influential galactojournalist, he. Just how wealthy, we were not to learn for many weeks; just how influential, I found out only five days ago.

As we wandered among the olive groves gone wild, picked our way through the ruins of the Frankish castle, or mixed our tracks with the hieroglyph-prints of the herring-gulls, there on the wet sands of the beaches of Kos, we were burning time while waiting for a ransom which could not come, which should never, really, have been expected.

Cassandra's hair is the color of Katamara olives, and shiny. Her hands are soft, the fingers short, delicately webbed. Her eyes are very dark. She is only about four inches shorter than me, which makes her gracefulness something of an achievement, me being well over six feet. Of course, any woman looks graceful, precise and handsome when walking at my side, because I am none of these things: my left cheek was then a map of Africa done up in varying purples, because of that mutant fungus I'd picked up from a moldy canvas back when I'd been disinterring the Guggenheim for the New York Tour; my hairline peaks to within a fingerbreadth of my brow; my eyes are mismatched. (I glare at people through the cold blue one on the right side when I want to intimidate them; the brown one is for Glances Sincere and Honest.) I wear a reinforced boot because of my short right leg.

Cassandra doesn't require contrasting, though. She's beautiful.

I met her by accident, pursued her with desperation, married her against my will. (The last part was her idea). I wasn't really thinking about it, myself—even on that day when I brought my caique into the harbor and saw her there, sunning herself like a mermaid beside the plane tree of Hippocrates, and decided that I wanted her. Kallikanzaroi have never been much the family sort. I just sort of slipped up, again.

It was a clean morning. It was starting our third month together. It was my last day on Kos—because of a call I'd received the evening before. Everything was still moist from the night's rain, and we sat out on the patio drinking Turkish coffee and eating oranges. Day was starting to lever its way into the world. The breeze was intermittent, was damp, goosepimpled us beneath the black hulk of our sweaters, skimmed the steam off the top of the coffee.

"Rodos dactylos Aurora. . . ." she said, pointing.

"Yeah," I said, nodding, "real rosy-fingered and nice."

"Let's enjoy it."

"Yeah. Sorry."

We finished our coffee, sat smoking.

"I feel crummy," I said.

"I know," she said. "Don't."

"Can't help it. Got to go away and leave you, and that's crummy."

"It may only be a few weeks. You said so yourself. Then you'll be back."

"Hope so," I said. "If it takes any longer, though, I'll send for you. Dunno where all I'll be, yet."

"Who is Cort Myshtigo?"

"Vegan actor, journalist. Important one. Wants to write about what's left of Earth. So I've got to show it to him. Me. Personally. Damn!"

"Anybody who takes ten-month vacations to go sailing can't complain about being overworked."

"*I* can complain—and I will. My job is supposed to be a sinecure."

"Why?"

"Mainly because I made it that way. I worked hard for twenty years to make Arts, Monuments and Archives what it is, and ten years ago I got it to the point where my staff could handle just about everything. So I got me turned out to pasture, I got me told to come back occasionally to sign papers and to do whatever I damn pleased in the meantime. Now this—this bootlicking gesture!—having a Commissioner take a Vegan scribbler on a tour any staff guide could conduct! Vegans aren't gods!"

"Wait a minute, please," she said. "Twenty years? Ten years?"

Sinking feeling.

"You're not even thirty years old."

I sank further. I waited. I rose again.

"Uh—there's something I, well, in my own reticent way, sort of never quite got around to mentioning to you. . . . How old are you anyway, Cassandra?"

"Twenty."

"Uh-huh. Well . . . I'm around four times your age."

"I don't understand."

"Neither do I. Or the doctors. I just sort of stopped, somewhere between twenty and thirty, and I stayed that way. I guess that's a sort of, well—a part of my particular mutation, I guess. Does it make any difference?"

"I don't know. . . . Yes."

"You don't mind my limp, or my excessive shagginess, or even my face. Why should my age bother you? I *am* young, for all necessary purposes."

"It's just that it's not the same," she said with an unarguable finality. "What if you never grow old?"

I bit my lip. "I'm bound to, sooner or later."

"And if it's later? I love you. I don't want to outage you."

"You'll live to be a hundred and fifty. There are the S-S treatments. You'll have them."

"But they won't keep me young—like you."

"I'm not really young. I was born old."

That one didn't work either. She started to cry.

"That's years and years away," I told her. "Who knows what will happen in the meantime?"

That only made her cry more.

I've always been impulsive. My thinking is usually pretty good, but I always seem to do it after I do my talking—by which time I've generally destroyed all basis for further conversation.

Which is one of the reasons I have a competent staff, a good radio, and am out to pasture most of the time.

There are some things you just can't delegate, though.

So I said, "Look, you have a touch of the Hot Stuff in you, too. It took me forty years to realize I wasn't forty years old. Maybe you're the same way. I'm just a neighborhood kid . . ."

"Do you know of any other cases like your own?"

"Well . . ."

"No, you don't."

"No, I don't."

I remember wishing then that I was back aboard my ship. Not the big blazeboat. Just my old hulk, the *Golden Vanitie,* out there in the harbor. I remember wishing that I was putting it into port all over again, and seeing her there for the first shiny time, and being able to start everything all over again from the beginning—and either telling her all about it right there, or else working my way back up to the going-away time and keeping my mouth shut about my age.

It was a nice dream, but hell, the honeymoon was over.

I waited until she had stopped crying and I could feel her eyes on me again. Then I waited some more.

"Well?" I asked, finally.

"Pretty well, thanks."

I found and held her passive hand, raised it to my lips. "Rodos dactylos," I breathed, and she said, "Maybe it's a good idea—your going away—for awhile anyhow. . . ." and the breeze that skimmed the steam came again, was damp, goosepimpled us, and made either her hand or my hand shake—I'm not sure which. It shook the leaves too, and they emptied over our heads.

"Did you exaggerate your age to me?" she asked. "Even a little bit?"

Her tone of voice suggested that agreement would be the wisest reply.

So, "Yes," I said, truthfully.

She smiled back then, somewhat reassured of my humanity.

Ha!

So we sat there, holding hands and watching the morning. After awhile she began humming. It was a sad song, centuries old. A ballad. It told the story of a young wrestler named Themocles, a wrestler who had never been beaten. He eventually came to consider himself the greatest wrestler alive. Finally he called out his challenge from a mountaintop, and, that being too near home, the gods acted fast: the following day a crippled boy rode into the town, on the plated back of a huge wild dog. They wrestled for three days and three nights. Themocles and the boy, and on the fourth day the boy broke his back, and left him there in the field. Wherever his blood fell, there sprang up the *strigefleur*, as Emmet calls it, the blood-drinking flower that creeps rootless at night, seeking the lost spirit of the fallen champion in the blood of its victims. But Themocles' spirit is gone from the Earth, so they must creep, seeking, forever. Simpler than Aeschylus, but then we're a simpler people than we once were, especially the Mainlanders. Besides, that's not the way it really happened.

"Why are you weeping?" she asked me suddenly.

"I am thinking of the picture on Achilleus' shield," I said, "and of what a terrible thing it is to be an educated beast—and I am not weeping. The leaves are dripping on me."

"I'll make some more coffee."

I washed out the cups while she was doing that, and I told her to take care of the *Vanitie* while I was gone, and to have it hauled up into drydock if I sent for her. She said that she would.

The sun wandered up higher into the sky, and after a time there came a sound of hammering from the yard of old Aldones, the coffin-maker. The cyclamen had come awake, and the breezes carried their fragrance to us from across the fields. High overhead, like a dark omen, a spiderbat glided across the sky toward the mainland. I ached to wrap my fingers around the stock of a thirty-oh-six, make loud noises, and watch it fall. The only firearms I knew of were aboard the *Vanitie,* though, so I just watched it vanish from sight.

"They say that they're not really native to Earth," she told me, watching it go, "and that they were brought here from Titan, for zoos and things like that."

"That's right."

". . . And that they got loose during the Three Days and went wild, and that they grow bigger here than they ever did on their own world."

"One time I saw one with a thirty-two foot wingspread."

"My great-uncle once told me a story he had heard in Athens," she recalled, "about a man killing one without any weapons. It snatched him up from the dock he was standing on—at Piraeus—

and the man broke its neck with his hands. They fell about a hundred feet into the bay. The man lived."

"That was a long time ago," I remembered, "back before the Office started its campaign to exterminate the things. They were a lot more around, and they were bolder in those days. They shy away from cities now."

"The man's name was Konstantin, as I recall the story. Could it have been you?"

"His last name was Karaghiosis."

"Are you Karaghiosis?"

"If you want me to be. Why?"

"Because he later helped to found the Returnist Radpol in Athens, and you have very strong hands."

"Are you a Returnist?"

"Yes. Are you?"

"I work for the Office. I don't have any political opinions."

"Karaghiosis bombed resorts."

"So he did."

"Are you sorry he bombed them?"

"No."

"I don't really know much about you, do I?"

"You know anything about me. Just ask. I'm really quite simple. —My air taxi is coming now."

"I don't hear anything."

"You will."

After a moment it came sliding down the sky toward Kos, homing in on the beacon I had set up at the end of the patio. I stood and drew her to her feet as it buzzed in low—a Radson Skimmer: a twenty-foot cockleshell of reflection and transparency; flat-bottomed, blunt-nosed.

"Anything you want to take with you?" she asked.

"You know it, but I can't."

The Skimmer settled and its side slid open. The goggled pilot turned his head.

"I have a feeling," she said, "that you are heading into some sort of danger."

"I doubt it, Cassandra."

Nor pressure, nor osmosis will restore Adam's lost rib, thank God.

"Goodbye, Cassandra."

"Goodbye, my kallikanzaros."

And I got into the Skimmer and jumped into the sky, breathing a prayer to Aphrodite. Below me, Cassandra waved. Behind me, the sun tightened its net of light. We sped westward, and this is the place for a smooth transition, but there isn't any. From Kos to Port-au-Prince was four hours, gray water, pale stars, and me mad. Watch the colored lights. . . .

The hall was lousy with people, a big tropical moon was shining fit to bust, and the reason I could see both was that I'd finally managed to lure Ellen Emmet out onto the balcony and the doors were mag-pegged open.

"Back from the dead again," she had greeted me, smiling slightly. "Gone almost a year, and not so much as a Get Well card from Ceylon."

"Were you ill?"

"I could have been."

She was small and, like all day-haters, creamy somewhere under her simicolor. She reminded me of an elaborate actiondoll with a faulty mechanism —cold grace, and a propensity to kick people in the shins when they least expected it; and she had lots and lots of orangebrown hair, woven into a Gordian knot of a coiff that frustrated me as I worked at untying it, mentally; her eyes were of whatever color it pleased the god of her choice on that particular day —I forget now, but they're always blue somewhere deep deep down inside. Whatever she was wearing was browngreen, and there was enough of it to go around a couple of times and make her look like a shapeless weed, which was a dressmaker's lie if there ever was one, unless she was pregnant again, which I doubted.

"Well, get well," I said, "if you need to. I didn't make Ceylon. I was in the Mediterranean most of the time."

There was applause within. I was glad I was without. The players had just finished Graber's *Masque of Demeter,* which he had written in pentameter and honor of our Vegan guest; and the thing had been two hours long, and bad. Phil was all educated and sparsehaired, and he looked the part all right, but we had been pretty hard up for a laureate on the day we'd picked him. He was given to fits of Rabindranath Tagore and Chris Isherwood, the writing of fearfully long metaphysical epics, talking a lot about Enlightenment, and performing his daily breathing exercises on the beach. Otherwise, he was a fairly decent human being.

The applause died down, and I heard the glassy tinkle of thelinstra music and the sound of resuming voices.

Ellen leaned back on the railing.

"I hear you're somewhat married these days."

"True," I agreed; "also somewhat harried. Why did they call me back?"

"Ask your boss."

"I did. He said I'm going to be a guide. What I want to know, though, is *why?* —The real reason. I've been thinking about it and it's grown more puzzling."

"So how should I know?"

"You know everything."

"You overestimate me, dear. What's she like?"

I shrugged.

"A mermaid, maybe. Why?"

She shrugged.

"Just curious. What do you tell people I'm like?"

"I don't tell people you're like anything."

"I'm insulted. I must be like something, unless I'm unique."

"That's it, you're unique."

"Then why didn't you take me away with you last year?"

"Because you're a People person and you require a city around you. You could only be happy here at the Port."

"But I'm *not* happy here at the Port."

"You are less unhappy here at the Port than you'd be anywhere else on this planet."

"We could have tried," she said, and she turned her back on me to look down the slope toward the lights of the harbor section.

"You know," she said after a time, "You're so damned ugly you're attractive. That must be it."

I stopped in mid-reach, a couple inches from her shoulder.

"You know," she continued, her voice flat, emptied of emotion, "you're a nightmare that walks like a man."

I dropped my hand, chuckled inside a tight chest.

"I know," I said. "Pleasant dreams."

I started to turn away and she caught my sleeve.

"Wait!"

I looked down at her hand, up at her eyes, then back down at her hand. She let go.

"You know I never tell the truth," she said. Then she laughed her little brittle laugh.

". . . And I *have* thought of something you ought to know about this trip. Donald Dos Santos is here, and I think he's going along."

"Dos Santos? That's ridiculous."

"He's up in the library now, with George and some big Arab."

I looked past her and down into the harbor section, watching the shadows, like my thoughts, move along dim streets, dark and slow.

"Big Arab?" I said, after a time. "Scarred hands? Yellow Eyes?—Name of Hasan?"

"Yes, that's right. Have you met him?"

"He's done some work for me in the past," I acknowledged.

So I smiled, even though my blood was refrigerating, because I don't like people to know what I'm thinking.

"You're smiling," she said. "What are you thinking?"

She's like that.

"I'm thinking you take things more seriously than I thought you took things."

"Nonsense. I've often told you I'm a fearful liar. Just a second ago, in fact—and I was only referring to a minor encounter in a great war. And you're right about my being less unhappy here than anywhere else on Earth. So maybe you could talk to George—get him to take a job on Taler, or Bakab. Maybe? Huh?"

"Yeah," I said. "Sure. You bet. Just like that. After you've tried it for ten years. —How *is* his bug collection these days?"

She sort of smiled.

"Growing," she replied, "by leaps and bounds. Buzzes and crawls too—and some of those crawlies are radioactive. I say to him, 'George, why don't you run around with other women instead of spending all your time with those bugs?' But he just shakes his head and looks dedicated. Then I say, 'George, one day one of those uglies is going to bite you and make you impotent. What'll you do then?' Then he explains that that can't happen, and he lectures me on insect toxins. Maybe he's really a big bug himself, in disguise. I think he gets some kind of sexual pleasure out of watching them swarm around in those tanks. I don't know what else—"

I turned away and looked inside the hall then, because her face was no longer *her* face. When I heard her laugh a moment later I turned back and squeezed her shoulder.

"Okay, I know more than I knew before. Thanks. I'll see you sometime soon."

"Should I wait?"

"No. Good night."

"Good night, Conrad."

And I was away.

Crossing a room can be a ticklish and time-consuming business: if it's full of people, if the people all know you, if the people are all holding glasses, if you have even a slight tendency to limp.

It was, they did and they were, and I do. So . . .

Thinking inconspicuous thoughts, I edged my way along the wall just at the periphery of humanity for about twenty feet, until I reached the enclave of young ladies the old celibate always has hovering about him. He was chinless, nearly lipless, and going hairless; and the expression that had once lived in that flesh covering his skull had long ago retreated into the darkness of his eyes, and the eyes had it as they caught me—the smile of imminent outrage.

"Phil," I said, nodding, "not everybody can write a masque like that. I've heard it said that it's a dying art, but now I know better."

"You're still alive," he said, in a voice seventy years younger than the rest of him, "and late again, as usual."

"I abase myself in my contrition," I told him, "but I was detained at a birthday party for a lady aged seven, at the home of an old friend." (Which was true, but it has nothing to do with this story.)

"All your friends are old friends, aren't they?" he asked, and that was hitting below the belt, just because I had once known his barely-remembered parents, and had taken them around to the south side of the Erechtheum in order to show them the Porch of the Maidens and point out what Lord Elgin had done with the rest, all the while carrying their bright-eyed youngsters on my shoulders and telling him tales that were old when the place was built.

". . . And I need your help," I added, ignoring the jibe and gently pushing my way through the soft, pungent circle of femininity. "It'll take me all night to cross this hall to where Sands is holding court with the Vegan—pardon me, Miss—and I don't have all night. —Excuse me, ma'am.—So I want you to run interference for me."

"You're Nomikos!" breathed one little lovely, staring at my cheek. "I've always wanted to—"

I seized her hand, pressed it to my lips, noted that her Camille-ring was glowing pink, said, "—And negative Kismet, eh?" and dropped it.

"So how about it?" I asked Graber. "Get me from here to there in a minimum of time in your typical courtier-like fashion, with a running conversation that no one would dare interrupt. Okay? Let's run."

He nodded brusquely.

"Excuse me, ladies. I'll be back."

We started across the room, negotiating alleys of people. High overhead, the chandeliers drifted and turned like faceted satellites of ice. The thelinstra was an intelligent Aeolian harp, tossing its shards of song into the air—pieces of colored glass. The people buzzed and drifted like certain of George Emmet's insects, and we avoided their swarms by putting one foot in front of another without pause and making noises of our own. We didn't step on anybody who squashed.

The night was warm. Most of the men wore the featherweight, black dress-uniform which protocol dictates the Staff suffer at these functions. Those who didn't weren't Staff.

Uncomfortable despite their lightness, the Dress Blacks mag-bind down the sides, leaving a smooth front whereon is displayed a green-blue-gray-white Earth insignia, about three inches in diameter, high up on the left breast; below, the symbol of one's department is worn, followed by the rank-sigil; on the right side goes every blessed bit of chicken manure that can be dreamt up to fake dignity—this, by the highly imaginative Office of Awards, Furbishments, Insignia, Symbols and Heraldry (OAFISH, for short—its first Director appreciated his position). The collar has a tendency to become a garrot after the first ten minutes; at least mine does.

The ladies wore, or didn't, whatever they pleased, usually bright or accompanied by pastel simicoloring (unless they were Staff, in which case they were neatly packed into short-skirted Dress Blacks, but with bearable collars), which makes it somewhat easier to tell some of the keepers from the kept.

"I hear Dos Santos is here," I said.

"So he is."

"Why?"

"I don't really know, or care."

"Tsk and tsk. What happened to your wonderful political consciousness? The Department of Literary Criticism used to praise you for it."

"At any age, the smell of death becomes more and more unsettling each time it's encountered."

"And Dos Santos smells?"

"He tends to reek."

"I've heard that he's employed a former associate of ours—from the days of the Madagascar Affair."

Phil cocked his head to one side and shot me a quizzical look.

"You hear things quite quickly. But then, you're a friend of Ellen's. Yes, Hasan is here. He's upstairs with Don."

"Whose karmic burden is he likely to help lighten?"

"As I said before, I don't really know or care about any of this."

"Want to venture a guess?"

"Not especially."

We entered a thinly-wooded section of the forest, and I paused to grab a rum-and-other from the dip-tray which had followed overhead until I could bear its anguish no longer, and had finally pressed the acorn which hung at the end of its tail. At this, it had dipped obligingly, smiled open, and revealed the treasures of its frosty interior.

"Ah, joy! Buy you a drink, Phil?"

"I thought you were in a hurry."

"I am, but I want to survey the situation some."

"Very well. I'll have a simicoke."

I squinted at him, passed him the thing. Then, as he turned away, I followed the direction of his gaze towards the easy chairs set in the alcove formed by the northeast corner of the room on two sides and the bulk of the thelinstra on the third. The thelinstra-player was an old lady with dreamy eyes. Earthdirector Lorel Sands was smoking his pipe. . . .

Now, the pipe is one of the more interesting facets of Lorel's personality. It's a real Meerschaum, and there aren't too many of them left in the world. As for the rest of him, his function is rather like that of an anticomputer: you feed him all kinds of carefully garnered facts, figures, and statistics and he translates them into garbage. Keen dark eyes, and a slow, rumbly way of speaking while he holds you with them; rarely given to gestures, but then very deliberate as he saws the air with a wide right hand or pokes imaginary ladies with his pipe; white at the temples and dark above; he is high of cheekbone, has a complexion that matches his tweeds (he assiduously avoids Dress Blacks), and he constantly strives to push his jaw an inch higher and further forward than seems comfortable. He is a political appointee, by the Earthgov on Taler, and he takes his work quite seriously, even to the extent of demonstrating his dedication with periodic attacks of ulcers. He is not the most intelligent man on Earth. He is my boss. He is also one of the best friends I have.

Beside him sat Cort Myshtigo. I could almost feel Phil hating him—from the pale blue soles of his six-toed feet to the pink upper-caste dye of his temple-to-temple hairstrip. Not hating him so much because he was him, but hating him, I was sure, because he was the closest available relative—grandson—of Tatram Yshtigo, who forty years before had commenced to demonstrate that the greatest living writer in the English language was a Vegan. The old gent is still at it, and I don't believe Phil has ever forgiven him.

Out of the corner of my eye (the blue one) I saw Ellen ascending the big, ornate stairway on the other side of the hall. Out of the other corner of my other eye I saw Lorel looking in my direction.

"I," said I, "have been spotted, and I must go now to pay my respects to the William Seabrook of Taler. Come along?"

"Well . . . Very well," said Phil; "suffering is good for the soul."

We moved on to the alcove and stood before the two chairs, between the music and the noise, there in the place of power. Lorel stood slowly and shook hands. Myshtigo stood more slowly, and did not shake hands; he stared, amber-eyed, his face expressionless as we were introduced. His loose-hanging orange shirt fluttered constantly as his chambered lungs forced their perpetual exhalation out the anterior nostrils at the base of his wide ribcage. He nodded briefly, repeated my name. Then he turned to Phil with something like a smile.

"Would you care to have me translate your masque into English?" he asked, his voice sounding like a dying-down tuning fork.

Phil turned on his heel and walked away.

Then I thought the Vegan was ill for a second, until I recollected that a Vegan's laugh sounds something like a billy goat choking. I try to stay away from Vegans by avoiding the resorts.

"Sit down," said Lorel, looking uncomfortable behind his pipe.

I drew up a chair and set it across from them.

"Okay."

"Cort is going to write a book," said Lorel.

"So you've said."

"About the Earth."

I nodded.

"He expressed a desire that you be his guide on a tour of certain of the Old Places. . . ."

"I am honored," I said rather stiffly. "Also, I am curious what determined his selection of me as guide."

"And even more curious as to what he may know about you, eh?" said the Vegan.

"Yes, I am," I agreed, "by a couple hundred percent."

"I asked a machine."

"Fine. Now I know."

I leaned back and finished my drink.

"I started by checking the Vite-Stats Register for Earth when I first conceived of this project—just for general human data—then, after I'd turned up an interesting item, I tried the Earthoffice Personnel Banks—"

"Mm-hm," I said.

"—and I was more impressed by what they did not say of you than by what they said."

I shrugged.

"There are many gaps in your career. Even now, no one really knows what you do most of the time."

"—And by the way, when were you born?"

"I don't know. It was in a tiny Greek village and they were all out of calendars that year. Christmas Day, though, I'm told."

"According to your personnel record, you're seventy-seven years old. According to Vite-Stats, you're either a hundred eleven or a hundred thirty."

"I fibbed about my age to get the job. There was a Depression going on."

"—So I made up a Nomikos-profile, which is a kind of distinctive thing, and I set Vite-Stats to hunting down .001 physical analogues in all of its banks, including the closed ones."

"Some people collect old coins, other people build model rockets."

"I found that you could have been three or four or five other persons, all of them Greeks, and one of them truly amazing. But, of course, Konstantin Korones, one of the older ones, was born two hundred thirty-four years ago. On Christmas. Blue eye, brown eye. Game right leg. Same hairline, at age twenty-three. Same height, and same Bertillion scales."

"Same fingerprints? Same retinal patterns?"

"These were not included in many of the older

Registry files. Maybe they were sloppier in those days? I don't know. More careless, perhaps, as to who had access to public records. . . ."

"You are aware that there are over four million persons on this planet right now. By searching back through the past three or four centuries I daresay you could find doubles, or even triples, for quite a few of them. So what?"

"It serves to make you somewhat intriguing, that's all, almost like a spirit of place—and you are as curiously ruined as this place is. Doubtless I shall never achieve your age, whatever it may be, and I was curious as to the sort of sensibilities a human might cultivate, given so much time—especially in view of your position as a master of your world's history and art.

"So that is why I asked for your services," he concluded.

"Now that you've met me, ruined and all, can I go home?"

"Conrad!" The pipe attacked me.

"No, Mister Nomikos, there are practical considerations also. This is a tough world, and you have a high survival potential. I want you with me because I want to survive."

I shrugged again.

"Well, that's settled. What now?"

He chuckled.

"I perceive that you dislike me."

"Whatever gave you that idea? Just because you insulted a friend of mine, asked me impertinent questions, impressed me into your service on a whim—"

"—exploited your countrymen, turned your world into a brothel, and demonstrated the utter provinciality of the human race, as compared to a galactic culture eons older. . . ."

"I'm not talking your race-my race. I'm talking personal talk. And I repeat, you insulted my friend, asked me impertinent questions, impressed me into your service on a whim."

"(*Billy goat snuffle*)! to all three!—It is an insult to the shades of Homer and Dante to have that man sing for the human race."

"At the moment he's the best we've got."

"In which case you should do without."

"That's no reason to treat him the way you did."

"I think it is, or I wouldn't have done it.—Second, I asked whatever questions I feel like asking, and it is your privilege to answer or not to answer as you see fit—just as you did.—Finally, nobody impressed you into anything. You are a civil servant. You have been given an assignment. Argue with your Office, not me.

"And, as an afterthought, I doubt that you possess sufficient data to use the word 'whim' as freely as you do," he finished.

From his expression, it appear that Lorel's ulcer was making silent commentary as I observed:

"Then call your rudeness plain dealing, if you will—or the product of another culture—and justify your influence with sophistries, and afterthink all you like—and by all means, deliver me all manner of spurious judgments, that I may judge you in return. You behave like a Royal Representative in a Crown Colony," I decided, pronouncing the capitals, "and I don't like it. I've read all your books. I've also read your granddad's—like his *Earthwhore's Lament*—and you'll never be the man he is. He has a thing called compassion. You don't. Anything you feel about old Phil goes double for you, in *my* book."

That part about grandpa must have touched on a sore spot, because he flinched when my blue gaze hit him.

"So kiss my elbow," I said, or something like that, in Vegan.

Sands doesn't speak enough Veggy to have caught it, but he made conciliatory noises immediately, looking about the while to be sure we were not being overhead.

"Conrad, please find your professional attitude and put it back on.—Srin Shtgio, why don't we get on with the planning?"

Myshtigo smiled his bluegreen smile.

"And minimize our differences?" he asked. "All right."

"Then let's adjourn to the library—where it's quieter—and we can use the map-screen."

"Fine."

I felt a bit reinforced as we rose to go, because Don Dos Santos was up there and he hates Vegans, and wherever Dos Santos is, there is always Diane, the girl with the red wig, and she hates everybody; and I knew George Emmet was upstairs, and Ellen, too—and George is a real cold fish around strangers (friends, too, for that matter); and perhaps Phil would wander in later and fire on Fort Sumter; and then there was Hasan—he doesn't say much, he just sits there and smokes his weeds and looks opaque—and if you stood too near him and took a couple deep breaths you wouldn't care what the hell you said to Vegans, or people either.

I had hoped that Hasan's memory would be on

the rocks, or else up there somewhere among the clouds.

Hope died as we entered the library. He was sitting straight and sipping lemonade.

Eighty or ninety or more, looking about forty, he could still act thirty. The Sprung-Samser treatments had found highly responsive material. It's not often that way. Almost never, in fact. They put some people into accelerated anaphylactic shock for no apparent reason, and even an intracardial blast of adrenalin won't haul them back; others, most others, they freeze at five or six decades. But some rare ones actually grow younger when they take the series—about one in a hundred thousand.

It struck me as odd that in destiny's big shooting gallery *this* one should make it, in such a way.

It had been over fifty years since the Madagascar Affair, in which Hasan had been employed by the Radpol in their vendetta against the Talerites. He had been in the pay of (Rest in Peace) the big K. in Athens, who had sent him to polish off the Earthgov Realty Company. He'd done it, too. And well. With one tiny fission device. Pow. Instant urban renewal. Called Hasan the Assassin by the Few, he is the last mercenary on Earth.

Also, besides Phil (who had not always been the wielder of the bladeless sword without a hilt), Hasan was one of the Very Few who could remember old Karaghios.

So, chin up and fungus forward, I tried to cloud his mind with my first glance. Either there were ancient and mysterious powers afoot, which I doubted, or he was higher than I'd thought, which was possible, or he had forgotten my face—which could have been possible, though not real likely—or he was exercising a professional ethic or a low animal cunning. (He possessed both of the latter, in varying degrees, but the accent was on the animal cunning.) He made no sign as we were introduced.

"My bodyguard, Hasan," said Dos Santos, flashing his magnesium-flare smile as I shook the hand that once had shaken the world, so to speak.

It was still a very strong hand.

"Conrad Nomikos," said Hasan, squinting as though he were reading it from off a scroll.

I knew everyone else in the room, so I hastened to the chair farthest from Hasan, and I kept my second drink in front of my face most of the time, just to be safe.

Diane of the Red Wig stood near. She spoke. She said, "Good morning, Mister Nomikos."

I nodded my drink.

"Good evening, Diane."

Tall, slim, wearing mostly white, she stood beside Dos Santos like a candle. I know it's a wig she wears, because I've seen it slip upwards on occasion, revealing part of an interesting and ugly scar which is usually hidden by the low hairline she keeps. I've often wondered about that scar, sometimes as I lay at anchor staring up at parts of constellations through clouds, or when I unearthed damaged statues. Purple lips—tattooed, I think—and I've never seen them smile; her jaw muscles are always raised cords because her teeth are always clenched; and there's a little upside-down "v" between her eyes, from all that frowning; and her chin is slight, held high—defiant? She barely moves her mouth when she speaks in that tight, choppy way of hers. I couldn't really guess at her age. Over thirty, that's all.

She and Don make an interesting pair. He is dark, loquacious, always smoking, unable to sit still for more than two minutes. She is taller by about five inches, burns without flickering. I still don't know all of her story. I guess I never will.

She came over and stood beside my chair while Lorel was introducing Cort to Dos Santos.

"You," she said.

"Me," I said.

"—will conduct the tour."

"Everybody knows all about it but me," said I. "I don't suppose you could spare me a little of your knowledge on the matter?"

"No knowledge, no matter," said she.

"You sound like Phil," said I.

"Didn't mean to."

"You did, though. So why?"

"Why what?"

"Why you? Don? Here? Tonight?"

She touched her tongue to her upper lip, then pressed it hard, as though to squeeze out the grape-juice or keep in the words. Then she looked over at Don, but he was too far away to have heard, and he was looking in another direction anyhow. He was busy pouring Myshtigo a real Coke from the pitcher in the exec dip-tray. The Coke formula had been the archaeological find of the century, according to the Vegans. It was lost during the Three Days and recovered only a decade or so ago. There had been lots of simicokes around, but none of them have the same effect on Vegan metabolism as the real thing. "Earth's second contribution to galactic culture," one of their contemporary historians had called it. The first contribution of course, being a very fine new social problem of the sort that weary Vegan philosophers had been waiting around for generations to have happen.

Diane looked back.

"Don't know yet," she said. "Ask Don."

"I will."

I did, too. Later, though. And I wasn't disappointed, inasmuch as I expected nothing.

But, as I sat trying as hard as I could to eavesdrop, there was suddenly a sight-vision overlay, of the sort a shrink had once classified for me as a pseudotelepathic wish-fulfillment. It works like this:

I want to know what's going on somewhere. I have almost-sufficient information to guess. Therefore, I do. Only it comes on as though I am seeing it and hearing it through the eyes and ears of one of the parties involved. It's not real telepathy, though, I don't think, because it can sometimes be wrong. It sure seems real, though.

The shrink could tell me everything about it but why.

Which is how I
was standing in the middle of the room,
was staring at Myshtigo,
was Dos Santos,
was saying:

". . . will be going along, for your protection. Not as Radpol Secretary, just a private citizen."

"I did not solicit your protection," the Vegan was saying; "however, I thank you. I will accept your offer to circumvent my death at the hands of your comrades"—and he smiled as he said it—"if they should seek it during my travels. I doubt that they will, but I should be a fool to refuse the shield of Dos Santos."

"You are wise," we said, bowing slightly.

"Quite," said Cort. "Now tell me"—he nodded toward Ellen, who had just finished arguing with George about anything and was stamping away from him—"who is that?"

"Ellen Emmet, the wife of George Emmet, the Director of the Wildlife Conservation Department."

"What is her price?"

"I don't know that she's quoted one recently."

"Well, what did it used to be?"

"There never was one."

"Everything on Earth has a price."

"In that case, I suppose you'll have to find out for yourself."

"I will," he said.

Earth femmes have always held an odd attraction for Vegans. A Veggy once told me that they make him feel rather like a zoophilist. Which is interesting, because a pleasure girl at the Cote d'Ôr Resort once told me, with a giggle, that Vegans made her feel rather like *une zoophiliste*. I guess those jets of air must tickle or something and arouse both beasts.

"By the way," we said, "have you stopped beating your wife lately?"

"Which one?" asked Myshtigo.

Fadeout, and me back in my chair.

". . . What," George Emmet was asking, "do you think of that?"

I stared at him. He hadn't been there a second ago. He had come up suddenly and perched himself on the wide wing of my chair.

"Come again, please. I was dozing."

"I said we've beaten the spiderbat. What do you think of that?"

"It rhymes," I observed. "So tell me how we've beaten the spiderbat."

But he was laughing. He's one of those guys with whom laughter is an unpredictable thing. He'll go around looking sour for days, and then some little thing will set him off giggling. He sort of gasps when he laughs, like a baby, and that impression is reinforced by his pink flaccidity and thinning hair. So I waited. Ellen was off insulting Lorel now, and Diane had turned to read the titles on the bookshelves.

Finally, "I've developed a new strain of *slishi,*" he panted confidentially.

"Say, that's really great!"

Then, "What are *slishi?*" I asked softly.

"The *slish* is a Bakabian parasite," he explained, "rather like a large tick. Mine are about three-eithths of an inch long," he said proudly, "and they burrow deep into the flesh and give off a highly poisonous waste product."

"Fatal?"

"Mine are."

"Could you lend me one?" I asked him.

"Why?"

"I want to drop it down someone's back. On second thought, make it a couple dozen. I have lots of friends."

"Mine won't bother people, just spiderbats. They discriminate against people. People would poison my *slishi.*" (He said "My *slishi*" very possessively.) "Their host has to have a copper- rather than an iron-based metabolism," he explained, "and spiderbats fall into that category. That's why I want to go with you on this trip."

"You want me to find a spiderbat and hold it for you while you dump *slishi* on it? Is that what you're trying to say?"

"Well, I *would* like a couple spiderbats to keep—I used all mine up last month—but I'm already sure the *slishi* will work. I want to go along to start the plague."

"Which plague?"

"Among the 'bats.—The *slishi* multiply quite rapidly under Earth conditions, if they're given the proper host, and they should be extremely contagious if we could get them started at the right time of year. What I had in mind was the late southwestern spiderbat mating season. It will begin in six to eight weeks in the territory of California, in an Old Place—not real hot anymore, though—called Capistrano. I understand that your tour will take you out that way at about that time. When the spiderbats return to Capistrano I want to be waiting for them with the *slishi*. Also, I could use a vacation."

"Mm-hm. Have you talked this over with Lorel?"

"Yes, and he thinks it's a fine idea. In fact, he wants to meet us out there and take pictures. There may not be too many more opportunities to see them—darkening the sky with their flight, nesting about the ruins the way they do, eating the wild pigs, leaving their green droppings in the streets—it's rather beautiful, you know."

"Uh-huh, sort of like Halloween. What'll happen to all those wild pigs if we kill off the spiderbats?"

"Oh, there'll be more of them around. But I figure the pumas will keep them from getting like Australian rabbits. Anyway, you'd rather have pigs than spiderbats, wouldn't you?"

"I'm not particularly fond of either, but now that I think of it I suppose I would rather have pigs than spiderbats. All right, sure, you can come along."

"Thank you," he said. "I was sure you'd help."

"Don't mention it."

Lorel made apologetic sounds deep in his throat about then. He stood beside the big desk in the middle of the room, before which the broad viewscreen was slowly lowering itself. It was a thick depth-transparer, so nobody had to move around after a better seat. He pressed a button on the side of the desk and the lights dimmed somewhat.

"Uh, I'm about to project a series of maps," he said, "if I can get this synchro-thing . . . There. There it is."

The upper part of Africa and most of the Mediterranean countries appeared in pastels.

"Is that the one you wanted first," he asked Myshtigo.

"It *was*—eventually," said the big Vegan, turning away from a muffled conversation with Ellen, whom he had cornered in the French History alcove beneath a bust of Voltaire.

The lights dimmed some more and Myshtigo moved to the desk. He looked at the map, and then at nobody in particular.

"I want to visit certain key sites which, for one reason or another, are important in the history of your world," he said. "I'd like to start with Egypt, Greece and Rome. Then I'd like to move on quickly through Madrid, Paris and London." The maps shifted as he talked, not fast enough, though, to keep up with him. "Then I want to backtrack to Berlin, hit Brussels, visit St. Petersburg and Moscow, skip back over the Atlantic and stop at Boston, New York, Dee-Cee, Chicago," (Lorel was working up a sweat by then) "drop down to Yucatan, and jump back up to the California territory."

"In that order?" I asked.

"Pretty much so," he said.

"What's wrong with India and the middle East—or the Far East, for that matter?" asked a voice which I recognized as Phil's. He had come in after the lights had gone down low.

"Nothing," said Myshtigo, "except that it's mainly mud and sand and hot, and has nothing whatsoever to do with what I'm after."

"What *are* you after?"

"A story."

"What kind of story?"

"I'll send you an autographed copy."

"Thanks."

"Your pleasure."

"When do you wish to leave?" I asked him.

"Day after tomorrow," he said.

"Okay."

"I've had detailed maps of the specific sites made up for you. Lorel tells me they were delivered to your office this afternoon."

"Okay again. But there is something of which you may not be fully cognizant. It involves the fact that everything you've named so far is mainlandish. We're pretty much an island culture these days, and for very good reasons. During the Three Days the Mainland got a good juicing, and most of the places you've named are still inclined to be somewhat hot. This, though, is not the only reason they are considered unsafe . . ."

"I am not unfamiliar with your history and I am

aware of the radiation precautions," he interrupted. "Also, I am aware of the variety of mutated life forms which inhabit Old Places. I am concerned, but not worried."

I shrugged in the artificial twilight.

"It's okay by me . . ."

"Good." He took another sip of Coke. "Let me have a little light then, Lorel."

"Right, Srin."

It was light again.

As the screen was sucked upward behind him, Myshtigo asked me, "Is it true that you are acquainted with several *mambos* and houngans here at the Port?"

"Why, yes," I said. "Why?"

He approached my chair.

"I understand," he said conversationally, "that voodoo, or *voudoun,* has survived pretty much unchanged over the centuries."

"Perhaps," I said. "I wasn't around here when it got started, so I wouldn't know for sure."

"I understand that the participants do not much appreciate the presence of outsiders—"

"That too, is correct. But they'll put on a good show for you, if you pick the right *hounfor* and drop in on them with a few gifts."

"But I should like very much to witness a real ceremony. If I were to attend one with someone who was not a stranger to the participants, perhaps then I could obtain the genuine thing."

"Why should you want to? Morbid curiosity concerning barbaric customs?"

"No. I am a student of comparative religions."

I studied his face, but couldn't tell anything from it.

It had been awhile since I'd visited with Mama Julie and Papa Joe or any of the others, and the *hounfor* wasn't that far away, but I didn't know how they'd take to me bringing a Vegan around. They'd never objected when I'd brought people, of course.

"Well . . ." I began.

"I just want to watch," he said. "I'll stay out of the way. They'll hardly know I'm there."

I mumbled a bit and finally gave in. I knew Mama Julie pretty well and I didn't see any real harm being done, no matter what.

So, "Okay," said I, "I'll take you to one. Tonight, if you like."

He agreed, thanked me, and went off after another Coke. George, who had not strayed from the arm of my chair, leaned toward me and observed that it would be very interesting to dissect a Vegan. I agreed with him.

When Myshtigo returned, Dos Santos was at his side.

"What is this about you taking Mister Myshtigo to a pagan ceremony?" he asked, nostrils flared and quivering.

"That's right," I said, "I am."

"Not without a bodyguard you are not."

I turned both palms upward.

"I am capable of handling anything which might arise."

"Hasan and I will accompany you."

I was about to protest when Ellen insinuated herself between them.

"I want to go, too," she said. "I've never been to one."

I shrugged. If Dos Santos went, then Diane would go, too, which made for quite a few of us.

So one more wouldn't matter, shouldn't matter. It was ruined before it got started.

"Why not?" I said.

The *hounfor* was located down in the harbor section, possibly because it was dedicated to Agué Woyo, god of the sea. More likely, though, it was because Mama Julie's people had always been harbor people. Agué Woyo is not a jealous god, so lots of other deities are commemorated upon the walls in brilliant colors. There are more elaborate *hounfors* further inland, but they tend to be somewhat commercial.

Agué's big blazeboat was blue and orange and green and yellow and black, and it looked to be somewhat unseaworthy. Damballa Wedo, crimson, writhed and coiled his length across most of the opposite wall. Several big *rada* drums were being stroked rhythmically by Papa Joe, forward and to the right of the door through which we entered—the only door. Various Christian saints peered from behind unfathomable expressions at the bright hearts and cocks and graveyard crosses, flags, machetes and crossroads that clung to almost every inch of the walls about them—frozen into an after-the-hurricane surrealism by the ampoteric paints of Titan—and whether or not the saints approved one could never tell: they stared down through their cheap picture-frames as though they were windows onto an alien world.

The small altar bore numerous bottles of alcoholic beverages, gourds, sacred vessels for the spirits of the *loa,* charms, pipes, flags, depth photos of unknown persons and, among other things, a pack of cigarettes for Papa Legba.

A service was in progress when we were led in by a young *hounsi* named Luis. The room was about eight meters long and five wide, had a high ceiling, a dirt floor. Dancers moved about the central pole with slow, strutting steps. Their flesh was dark and it glistened in the dim light of the antique kerosene lamps. With our entry the room became crowded.

Mama Julie took my hand and smiled. She led me back to a place beside the altar and said, "Erzulie was kind."

I nodded.

"She likes you, Nomiko. You live long, you travel much, and you come back."

"Always," I said.

"Those people . . . ?"

She indicated my companions with a flick of her dark eyes.

"Friends. They would be no bother . . ."

She laughed as I said it. So did I.

"I will keep them out of your way if you let us remain. We will stay in the shadows at the sides of the room. If you tell me to take them away, I will. I see that you have already danced much, emptied many bottles . . ."

"Stay," she said. "Come talk with me during daylight sometime."

"I will."

She moved away then and they made room for her in the circle of dancers. She was quite large, though her voice was a small thing. She moved like a huge rubber doll, not without grace, stepping to the monotonous thunder of Papa Joe's drumming. After a time this sound filled everything—my head, the earth, the air—like maybe the whale's heartbeat had seemed to half-digested Jonah. I watched the dancers. And I watched those who watched the dancers.

I drank a pint of rum in an effort to catch up, but I couldn't. Myshtigo kept taking sips of Coke from a bottle he had brought along with him. No one noticed that he was blue, but then we had gotten there rather late and things were pretty well along the way to wherever they were going.

Red Wig stood in a corner looking supercilious and frightened. She was holding a bottle at her side, but that's where it stayed. Myshtigo was holding Ellen at his side, and that's where she stayed. Dos Santos stood beside the door and watched everybody—even me. Hasan, crouched against the righthand wall, was smoking a long-stemmed pipe with a small bowl. He appeared to be at peace.

Mama Julie, I guess it was, began to sing. Other voices picked it up:

Papa Legba, ouvri bayê!
Papa Legba, Attibon Legba, ouvri bayê pou pou passê!
Papa Legba . . .

This went on, and on and on. I began to feel drowsy. I drank more rum and felt thirstier and drank more rum.

I'm not sure how long we had been there when it happened. The dancers had been kissing the pole and singing and rattling gourds and pouring out waters, and a couple of the *hounsi* were acting possessed and talking incoherently, and the meal-design on the floor was all blurred, and there was lots of smoke in the air, and I was leaning back against the wall and I guess my eyes had been closed for a minute or two.

The sound came from an unexpected quarter.

Hasan screamed.

It was a long, wailing thing that brought me forward, then dizzily off balance, then back to the wall again, with a thump.

The drumming continued, not missing a single beat. Some of the dancers stopped, though, staring.

Hasan had gotten to his feet. His teeth were bared and his eyes were slits, and his face bore the ridges and valleys of exertion beneath its sheen of sweat.

His beard was a fireshot spearhead.

His cloak, caught high against some wall decoration, was black wings.

His hands, in a hypnosis of slow motion, were strangling a non-existent man.

Animal sounds came from his throat.

He continued to choke nobody.

Finally, he chuckled and his hands sprang open.

Dos Santos was at his side almost immediately, talking to him, but they inhabited two different worlds.

One of the dancers began to moan softly. Another joined him—and others.

Mama Julie detached herself from the circle and came toward me—just as Hasan started the whole thing over again, this time with more elaborate histrionics.

The drum continued its steady, earthdance pronouncement.

Papa Joe did not even look up.

"A bad sign," said Mama Julie. "What do you know of this man?"

"Plenty," I said, forcing my head to clear by an act of will.

"Angelsou," she said.

"What?"

"Angelsou," she repeated. "He is a dark god—one to be feared. Your friend is possessed by Angelsou."

"Explain, please."

"He comes seldom to our *hounfor*. He is not wanted here. Those he possesses become murderers."

"I think Hasan was trying a new pipe mixture—mutant ragweed or something."

"Angelsou," she said again. "Your friend will become a killer, for Angelsou is a deathgod, and he only visits with his own."

"Mama Julie," said I, "Hasan *is* a killer. If you had a piece of gum for every man he's killed and you tried to chew it all, you'd look like a chipmunk. He is a professional killer—within the limits of the law, usually. Since the Code Duello prevails on the Mainland, he does most of his work there. It has been rumored that he does an illegal killing on occasion, but this thing has never been proved.

"So tell me," I finished, "is Angelsou the god of killers or the god of murderers? There should be a difference between the two, shouldn't there?"

"Not to Angelsou," she said.

Dos Santos then, trying to stop the show, seized both of Hasan's wrists. He tried to pull his hands apart, but—well, try bending the bars of your cage sometime and you'll get the picture.

I crossed the room, as did several of the others. This proved fortunate, because Hasan had finally noticed that someone was standing in front of him, and dropped his hands, freeing them. Then he produced a long-bladed stiletto from under his cloak.

Whether or not he would actually have used it on Don or anybody else is a moot point, because at that moment Myshtigo stoppered his Coke bottle with his thumb and hit him behind the ear with it. Hasan fell forward and Don caught him, and I pried the blade from between his fingers, and Myshtigo finished his Coke.

"Interesting ceremony," observed the Vegan; "I would never have suspected that big fellow of harboring such strong religious feelings."

"It just goes to show you that you can never be too sure, doesn't it?"

"Yes." He gestured to indicate the onlookers. "They are all pantheists, aren't they?"

I shook my head. "Primitive animists."

"What is the difference?"

"Well, that Coke bottle you just emptied is going to occupy the altar, or *pé,* as it is called, as a vessel for Angelsou, since it has enjoyed an intimate mystical relationship with the god. That's the way an animist would see it. Now, a pantheist just might get a little upset at somebody's coming in to his ceremonies uninvited and creating a disturbance such as we just did. A pantheist might be moved to sacrifice the intruders to Agué Woyo, god of the sea, by hitting them all over the head in a similar ceremonial manner and tossing them off the end of the dock. Therefore, I am not going to have to explain to Mama Julie that all these people standing around glaring at us are really animists. Excuse me a minute."

It wasn't really that bad, but I wanted to shake him up a bit. I think I did.

After I'd apologized and said good-night, I picked up Hasan. He was out cold and I was the only one big enough to carry him.

The street was deserted except for us, and Agué Woyo's big blazeboat was cutting the waves somewhere just under the eastern edge of the world and splashing the sky with all his favorite colors.

Dos Santos, at my side, said, "Perhaps you were correct. Maybe we should not have come along."

I didn't bother to answer him, but Ellen, who was walking up ahead with Myshtigo, stopped, turned, and said, "Nonsense. If you hadn't, we would have missed the tentmaker's wonderful dramatic monologue." By then, I was within range and both her hands shot out and wrapped around my throat. She applied no pressure, but she grimaced horribly and observed, "Ur! Mm! Ugh! I'm possessed of Angelsou and you've had it." Then she laughed.

"Let go my throat or I'll throw this Arab at you," I said, comparing the orangebrown color of her hair with the orangepink color of the sky behind her, and smiled.

"He's a heavy one, too," I added.

Then, a second before she let go, she applied some pressure—a little bit too much to be playful—and then she was back on Myshtigo's arm and we were walking again. Well, women never slap me because I always turn the other cheek first and they're afraid of the fungus, so I guess a quick choke is about the only alternative.

"Frightfully interesting," said Red Wig. "Felt strange. As if something inside me was dancing along with them. Odd feeling, it was. I don't really like dancing—any kind."

"What kind of accent do you have?" I interrupted her. "I've been trying to place it."

"Don't know," she said. "I'm sort of Irish-French. Lived in the Hebrides—also Australia, Japan—till I was nineteen . . ."

Hasan moaned just then and flexed his muscles and I felt a sharp pain in my shoulder.

I set him down on a doorstep and shook him down. I found two throwing knives, another stiletto, a very neat gravity knife, a saw-edged Bowie, strangling wires, and a small metal case containing various powders and vials of liquids which I did not care to inspect too closely. I liked the gravity knife, so I kept it for myself. It was a Coricama, and very neat.

Late the next day—call it evening—I shanghaied old Phil, determined to use him as the price of admission to Dos Santos' suite at the *Royal*. The Radpol still reveres Phil as a sort of Returnist Tom Paine, even though he began pleading innocent to that about half a century ago, back when he began getting mysticism and respectability. While his *Call of Earth* probably *is* the best thing he ever wrote, he also drafted the Articles of Return, which helped to start the trouble I'd wanted started. He may do much disavowing these days, but he was a troublemaker then, and I'm sure he still files away all the fawning gazes and bright words it continues to bring him, takes them out every now and then, dusts them off, and regards them with something like pleasure.

Besides Phil, I took along a pretext—that I wanted to see how Hasan was feeling after the lamentable bash he'd received at the *hounfor*. Actually, what I wanted was a chance to talk to Hasan and find out how much, if anything, he'd be willing to tell me about his latest employment.

So Phil and I walked it. It wasn't far from the Office compound to the *Royal*. About seven minutes, ambling.

"Have you finished writing my elegy yet?" I asked.

"I'm still working on it."

"You've been saying that for the past twenty years. I wish you'd hurry up so I could read it."

"I could show you some very fine ones . . . Lorel's, George's, even one for Dos Santos. And I have all sorts of blank ones in my files—the fill-in kind—for lesser notables. Yours is a problem, though."

"How so?"

"I have to keep updating it. You go right on, quite blithely—living, doing things."

"You disapprove?"

"Most people have the decency to do things for half a century and then stay put. Their elegies present no problems. I have cabinets full. But I'm afraid yours is going to be a last-minute thing with a discord ending. I don't like to work that way. I prefer to deliberate over a span of many years, to evaluate a person's life carefully, and without pressure. You people who live your lives like folksongs trouble me. I think you're trying to force me to write you an epic, and I'm getting too old for that. I sometimes nod."

"I think you're being unfair," I told him. "Other people get to read their elegies, and I'd even settle for a couple of good limericks."

"Well, I have a feeling yours will be finished before too long," he noted. "I'll try to get a copy to you in time."

"Oh? From whence springs this feeling?"

"Who can isolate the source of an inspiration?"

"You tell me."

"It came upon me as I meditated. I was in the process of composing one for the Vegan—purely as an exercise, of course—and I found myself thinking: 'Soon I will finish the Greek's.'" After a moment, he continued, "Conceptualize this thing: yourself as two men, each taller than the other."

"It could be done if I stood in front of a mirror and kept shifting my weight. I have this short leg.—So, I'm conceptualizing it. What now?"

"Nothing. You don't go at these things properly."

"It's a cultural tradition against which I have never been successfully immunized. Like knots, horses—Gordia, Troy. You know. We're sneaky."

He was silent for the next ten paces.

"So feathers or lead?" I asked him.

"Pardon?"

"It is the riddle of the kallikanzaros. Pick one."

"Feathers?"

"You're wrong."

"If I had said 'lead' . . . ?"

"Uh-uh. You only have one chance. The correct answer is whatever the kallikanzaros wants it to be. You lose."

"That sounds a bit arbitrary."

"Kallikanzaroi are that way. It's Greek, rather than Oriental subtlety. Less inscrutable, too. Because your life often depends on the answer, and the kallikanzaros generally wants you to lose."

"Why is that?"

"Ask the next kallikanzaros you meet, if you get the chance. They're mean spirits."

We struck the proper avenue and turned up it.

"Why are you suddenly concerned with the Rad-pol again?" he asked. "It's been a long time since you left."

"I left at the proper time, and all I'm concerned with is whether it's coming alive again—like in the old days. Hasan comes high because he always delivers, and I want to know what's in the package."

"Are you worried they've found you out?"

"No. It might be uncomfortable, but I doubt it would be incapacitating."

The *Royal* loomed before us and we entered. We went directly to the suite. As we walked up the padded hallway, Phil, in a fit of perception, observed, "I'm running interference again."

"That about says it."

"Okay. One'll get you ten you find out nothing."

"I won't take you up on that. You're probably right."

I knocked on the darkwood door.

"Hi there," I said as it opened.

"Come in, come in."

And we were off.

It took me ten minutes to turn the conversation to the lamentable bashing of the Bedouin, as Red Wig was there distracting me by being there and being distracting.

"Good morning," she said.

"Good evening," I said.

"Anything new happening in Arts?"

"No."

"Monuments?"

"No."

"Archives?"

"No."

"What interesting work you must do!"

"Oh, it's been overpublicized and glamorized all out of shape by a few romanticists in the Information Office. Actually, all we do is locate, restore, and preserve the records and artifacts mankind has left lying about the Earth."

"Sort of like cultural garbage collectors?"

"Mm, yes. I think that's properly put."

"Well, why?"

"Why what?"

"Why do you do it?"

"Someone has to, because it's cultural garbage. That makes it worth collecting. I know my garbage better than anyone else on Earth."

"You're dedicated, as well as being modest. That's good, too."

"Also, there weren't too many people to choose from when I applied for the job—and I knew where a lot of the garbage was stashed." She handed me a drink, took a sip and a half of her own, and asked, "Are they actually still around?"

"Who?" I inquired.

"Divinity Incorporated. The old gods. Like Angelsou. I thought all the gods had left the Earth."

"No, they didn't. Just because most of them resemble us doesn't mean they act the same way. When man left he didn't offer to take them along, and gods have some pride, too. But then, maybe they had to stay, anyhow—that thing called *ananke*, death-destiny. Nobody prevails against it."

"Like progress?"

"Yeah. Speaking of progress, how is Hasan progressing? The last time I saw him he had stopped entirely."

"Up, around. Big lump. Thick skull. No harm."

"Where is he?"

"Up the hall, left. Games Room."

"I believe I'll go render him my sympathy. Excuse me?"

"Excused," she said, nodding, and she went away to listen to Dos Santos talk at Phil. Phil, of course, welcomed the addition.

Neither looked up as I left.

The Games Room was at the other end of the long hallway. As I approached, I heard a *thunk* followed by a silence, followed by another *thunk*.

I opened the door and looked inside.

He was the only one there. His back was to me, but he heard the door open and turned quickly. He was wearing a long purple dressing gown and was balancing a knife in his right hand. There was a big wad of plastage on the back of his head.

"Good evening, Hasan."

A tray of knives stood at his side, and he had set a target upon the opposite wall. Two blades were sticking into the target—one in the center and one about six inches off, at nine o'clock.

"Good evening," he said slowly. Then, after thinking it over, he added, "How are you?"

"Oh, fine. I came to ask you that same question. How is your head?"

"The pain is great, but it shall pass."

I closed the door behind me.

"You must have been having quite a daydream last night."

"Yes. Mister Dos Santos tells me I fought with ghosts. I do not remember."

"You weren't smoking what the fat Doctor Emmet would call Cannabis sativa, that's for sure."

"No, Karagee. I smoked a stirge-fleur which had

drunk human blood. I found it near the Old Place of Constantinople and dried its blossoms carefully. An old woman told me it would give me sight into the future. She lied."

". . . And the vampire-blood incites to violence? Well, that's a new one to write down. By the way, you just called me Karagee. I wish you wouldn't. My name is Nomikos, Conrad Nomikos."

"Yes, Karagee. I was surprised to see you. I had thought you died long ago, when your blazeboat broke up in the bay."

"Karagee did die then. You have not mentioned to anyone that I resemble him, have you?"

"No; I do not make idle talk."

"That's a good habit."

I crossed the room, selected a knife, weighed it, threw it, and laid it about ten inches to the right of center.

"Have you been working for Mister Dos Santos very long?" I asked him.

"For about the period of a month," he replied.

He threw his knife. It struck five inches below the center.

"You are his bodyguard, eh?"

"That is right. I also guard the blue one."

"Don says he fears an attempt on Myshtigo's life. Is there an actual threat, or is he just being safe?"

"It is possible either way, Karagee. I do not know. He pays me only to guard."

"If I paid you more, would you tell me whom you've been hired to kill?"

"I have only been hired to guard, but I would not tell you even if it were otherwise."

"I didn't think so. Let's go get the knives."

We crossed and drew the blades from the target.

"Now, if it happens to be me—which is possible," I offered, "why don't we settle it right now? We are each holding two blades. The man who leaves this room will say that the other attacked him and that it was a matter of self-defense. There are no witnesses. We were both seen drunk or disorderly last night."

"No, Karagee."

"No, what? No, it isn't me? Or no, you don't want to do it that way?"

"I could say no, it is not you. But you would not know whether I spoke the truth or not."

"That is true."

"I could say I do not want to do it that way."

"Is that true?"

"I do not say. But to give you the satisfaction of an answer, what I will say is this: If I wished to kill you, I would not attempt it with a knife in my hand, nor would I box nor wrestle with you."

"Why is that?"

"Because many years ago when I was a boy I worked at the Resort of Kerch, attending at the tables of the wealthy Vegans. You did not know me then. I had just come up from the places of Pamir. You and your friend the poet came to Kerch."

"I remember now. Yes . . . Phil's parents had died that year—they were good friends of mine—and I was going to take Phil to the university. But there was a Vegan who had taken his first woman from him, taken her to Kerch. Yes, the entertainer —I forget his name."

"He was Thrilpai Ligo, the shajadpa-boxer, and he looked like a mountain at the end of a great plain —high, immovable. He boxed with the Vegan cesti —the leather strips with the ten sharpened studs that go all the way around the hand—open-handed."

"Yes, I remember. . . ."

"You had never boxed shajadpa before, but you fought with him for the girl. A great crowd came, of the Vegans and the Earth girls, and I stood on a table to watch. After a minute your head was all blood. He tried to make it run into your eyes, and you kept shaking your head. I was fifteen then and had only killed three men myself, and I thought that you were going to die because you had not even touched him. And then your right hand crossed to him like a thrown hammer, so fast! You struck him in the center of that double bone the blue ones have in their chests—and they are tougher there than we—and you crushed him like an egg. I could never have done that, I am sure—and that is why I fear your hands and your arms. Later, I learned that you had also broken a spiderbat.—No, Karagee, I would kill you from a distance."

"That was so long ago. . . . I did not think anyone remembered."

"You won the girl."

"Yes. I forget her name."

"But you did not give her back to the poet. You kept her for yourself. That is why he probably hates you."

"Phil? That girl? I've even forgotten what she looked like."

"He has never forgotten. That is why I think he hates you. I can smell hate, sniff out its sources. You took away his first woman. I was there."

"It was her idea."

". . . And he grows old and you stay young. It is

sad, Karagee, when a friend has reason to hate a friend."

"Yes."

"And I do not answer your questions."

"It is possible that you were hired to kill the Vegan."

"It is possible."

"Why?"

"I said only that it is possible, not that it is fact."

"Then I will ask you one more question only, and be done with it. What good would come of the Vegan's death? His book could be a very good thing in the way of Vegan-human relations."

"I do not know what good or bad would come of it, Karagee. Let us throw more knives."

We did. I picked up the range and the balance and put two right in the center of the target. Then Hasan squeezed two in beside them, the last one giving out the sharp paincry of metal as it vibrated against one of mine.

"I will tell you a thing," I said, as we drew them again. "I am head of the tour and responsible for the safety of its members. I, too, will guard the Vegan."

"That will be a very good thing, Karagee. He needs protecting."

I placed the knives back in the tray and moved to the door.

"We will be leaving at nine tomorrow morning, you know. I'll have a convoy of Skimmers at the first field in the Office compound."

"Yes. Good night, Karagee."

". . . And call me Conrad."

"Yes."

He had a knife ready to throw at the target. I closed the door and moved back up the corridor. As I went, I heard another *thunk,* and it sounded much closer than the first ones had. It echoed all around me, there in the hallway.

As the six big Skimmers fled across the oceans toward Egypt I turned my thoughts first to Kos and Cassandra and then dragged them back with some difficulty and sent them on ahead to the land of sand, the Nile, mutated crocs, and some dead Pharoahs whom one of my most current projects was then disturbing. ("Death comes on swift wings to he who defiles . . ." etc.), and I thought then of humanity, roughly ensconced on the Titan way-station, working in the Earth-office, abasing itself on Taler and Bakab, getting by on Mars, and doing so-so on Rylpah, Divbah, Litan and a couple dozen other worlds in the Vegan Combine. Then I thought about the Vegans.

The blueskinned folk with the funny names and the dimples like pock-marks had taken us in when we were cold, fed us when we were hungry. Yeah. They appreciated the fact that our Martian and Titanian colonies had suffered from nearly a century of sudden self-sufficiency—after the Three Days incident—before a workable interstellar vehicle had been developed. Like the boll weevil (Emmet tells me) we were just looking for a home, because we'd used up the one we had. Did the Vegans reach for the insecticide? No. Wise elder race that they are, they permitted us to settle among their worlds, to live and work in their landcities, their seacities. For even a culture as advanced as the Vegans' has some need for hand labor of the opposing thumb variety. Good domestic servants cannot be replaced by machines, nor can machine monitors, good gardeners, salt sea fisherfolk, subterranean and subsquean hazard workers, and ethnic entertainers of the alien variety. Admittedly, the presence of human dwelling places lowers the value of adjacent Vegan properties, but then, humans themselves compensate for it by contributing to the greater welfare.

Which thought brought me back to Earth. The Vegans had never seen a completely devastated civilization before, so they were fascinated by our home planet. Fascinated enough to tolerate our absentee government on Taler. Enough to buy Earthtour tickets to view the ruins. Even enough to buy property here and set up resorts. There *is* a certain kind of fascination to a planet that is run like a museum. (What was it James Joyce said about Rome?) Anyhow, dead Earth still brings its living grandchildren a small but appreciable revenue every Vegan fiscal year. That is why—the Office, Lorel, George, Phil, and all that.

Sort of why me, even.

Far below, the ocean was a bluegray rug being pulled out from beneath us. The dark continent replaced it. We raced on toward New Cairo.

We set down outside the city. There's no real airstrip. We just dropped all six Skimmers down in an empty field we used as one, and we posted George as a guard.

Old Cairo is still hot, but the people with whom one can do business live mainly in New Cairo, so things were pretty much okay for the tour. Myshtigo did want to see the mosque of Kait Bey in the City of the Dead, which had survived the Three

Days; he settled, though, for me taking him up in my Skimmer and flying in low, slow circles about it while he took photographs and did some peering. In the way of monuments, it was really the pyramids and Luxur, Karnak, and the Valley of Kings and the Valley of Queens that he wanted to see.

It was well that we viewed the mosque from the air. Dark shapes scurried below us, stopping only to hurl rocks up toward the ship.

"What are they?" asked Myshtigo.

"Hot Ones," said I. "Sort of human. They vary in size, shape, and meanness."

After circling for a time he was satisfied, and we returned to the field.

So, landing again beneath a glaring sun, we secured the final Skimmer and disembarked, moving across equal proportions of sand and broken pavement—two temporary tour assistants, me, Myshtigo, Dos Santos and Red Wig, Ellen, Hasan. Ellen had decided at the last minute to accompany her husband on the journey. There were fields of high, shiny sugar cane on both sides of the road. In a moment we had left them behind and were passing the low outbuildings of the city. The road widened. Here and there a palm tree cast some shade. Two great-eyed, brown-eyed children looked up as we passed. They had been watching a weary, six-legged cow turn a great *sakieh* wheel, in much the same way as cows have always turned great *sakieh* wheels hereabouts, only this one left more hoofprints.

My area supervisor, Rameses Smith, met us at the inn. He was big, his golden face tightly contained within a fine net of wrinkles; and he had the typical sad eyes, but his constant chuckle quickly offset them.

We sat sipping beer in the main hall of the inn while we waited for George. Local guards had been sent to relieve him.

"The work is progressing well," Rameses told me.

"Good," I said, somewhat pleased that no one had asked me what "the work" was. I wanted to surprise them.

"How is your wife, and the children?"

"They are fine," he stated.

"The new one?"

"He has survived—and without defect," he said proudly. "I sent my wife to Corsica until he was delivered. Here is his picture."

I pretended to study it, making the expected appreciative noises. Then, "Speaking of pictures," I said, "do you need any more equipment for the filming?"

"No, we are well-stocked. All goes well. When do you wish to view the work?"

"Just as soon as we have something to eat."

"Are you a Moslem?" interrupted Myshtigo.

"I am of the Coptic faith," replied Rameses, not smiling.

"Oh, really? That was the Monophysite heresy, was it not?"

"We do not consider ourselves heretics," said Rameses.

I sat there wondering if we Greeks had done the right thing in unleashing logic onto a hapless world, as Myshtigo launched into an amusing (to him) catalog of Christian heresies. In a fit of spite at having to guide a tour, I recorded them all in the Tour Log. Later, Lorel told me that it was a fine and well-kept document. Which just goes to show how nasty I must have felt at that moment. I even put in the bit about the accidental canonization of Buddha as St. Josaphat in the sixteenth century. Finally, as Myshtigo sat there mocking us, I realized I would either have to cut him down or change the subject. Not being a Christian myself, his theological comedy of errors did not poke me in the religious plexus. It bothered me, though, that a member of another race had gone to such trouble doing research to make us look like a pack of idiots.

Reconsidering the thing at this time, I know now that I was wrong. The success of the viewtape I was making then ("the word" which Rameses had referred to) bears out a more recent hypothesis of mine concerning the Vegans: They were so bloody bored with themselves and we were so novel that they seized upon our perennially popular problems and our classical problems, as well as the one we were currently presenting in the flesh. They engaged in massive speculation as to who really wrote Shakespeare's plays, whether or not Napoleon actually died on St. Helena, who were the first Europeans to set foot on North America, and if the books of Charles Fort indicated that Earth had been visited by an intelligent race unknown to them —and so on. High caste Vegan society just eats up our medieval theological debates, too. Funny.

"About your book, Srin Shtigo . . ." I interrupted.

My use of the honorific stopped him.

"Yes?" he answered.

"My impression," said I, "is that you do not wish

to discuss it at any length at this time. I respect this feeling, of course, but it places me in a slightly awkward position as head of this tour." We both knew I should have asked him in private, especially after his reply to Phil at the reception, but I was feeling cantankerous and wanted to let him know it, as well as to rechannel the talk. So, "I'm curious," I said, "whether it will be primarily a travelogue of the places we visit, or if you would like assistance in directing your attention to special local conditions of any sort—say, political, or current cultural items."

"I am primarily interested in writing a descriptive travelbook," he said, "but I will appreciate your comments as we go along. I thought that was your job, anyway. As it is, I do have a general awareness of Earth traditions and current affairs, and I'm not very much concerned with them."

Dos Santos, who was pacing and smoking as our meal was being prepared, stopped in mid-stride and said, "Srin Shtigo, what are your feelings toward the Returnist movement? Are you sympathetic with our aims? Or do you consider it a dead issue?"

"Yes," he replied, "to the latter. I believe that when one is dead one's only obligation then is to satisfy the consumer. I respect your aims, but I do not see how you can possibly hope to realize them. Why should your people give up the security they now possess to return to this place? Most of the members of the present generation have never even seen the Earth, except on tapes—and you must admit that they are hardly the most encouraging documents."

"I disagree with you," said Dos Santos, "and I

find your attitude dreadfully patrician."

"That is as it should be," replied Myshtigo.

George and the food arrived at about the same time. The waiters began serving the food.

"I should prefer to eat at a small table by myself," Dos Santos instructed a waiter.

"You are here because you asked to be here," I mentioned.

He stopped in mid-flight and cast a furtive look at Red Wig, who happened to be sitting at my right hand. I thought I detected an almost imperceptible movement of her head, first to the left, then to the right.

Dos Santos composed his features around a small smile and bowed slightly.

"Forgive my Latin temperament," he observed. "I should hardly expect to convert anyone to Returnism in five minutes—and it has always been difficult for me to conceal my feelings."

"That is somewhat obvious."

"I'm hungry," I said.

He seated himself across from us, next to George.

"Behold the Sphinx," said Red Wig, gesturing toward an etching on the far wall, "whose speech alternates between long periods of silence and an occasional riddle. Old as time. Highly respected. Doubtless senile. She keeps her mouth shut and waits. For what? Who knows?—Does your taste in art run to the monolithic, Srin Shtigo?"

"Occasionally," he observed, from my left.

Dos Santos glanced once, quickly, over his shoulder, then back at Diane. He said nothing.

I asked Red Wig to pass me the salt and she did. I really wanted to dump it on her, to make her stay put so that I could study her at my leisure, but I used it on the potatoes instead.

Behold the Sphinx, indeed!

High sun, short shadows, hot—that's how it was. I didn't want any sand-cars or Skimmers spoiling the scene, so I made everybody hike it. It wasn't that far, and I took a slightly roundabout way in order to achieve the calculated effect.

We walked a crooked mile, climbing some, dipping some. I confiscated George's butterfly net so as to prevent any annoying pauses as we passed by the several clover fields which lay along our route.

Walking backward through time, that's how it was—with bright birds flashing by (*clare! clare!*), and a couple camels appearing against the far horizon whenever we topped a small rise. (Camel outlines, really, done up in charcoal; but that's enough. Who cares about a camel's expressions? Not even other camels—not really. Sickening beasts. . . .) A short, swarthy woman trudged past us with a tall jar on her head. Myshtigo remarked on this fact to his pocket secretary. I nodded to the woman and spoke a greeting. The woman returned the greeting but did not nod back, naturally. Ellen, moist already, kept fanning herself with a big green feather triangle; Red Wig walked tall, tiny beads of perspiration seasoning her upper lip, eyes hidden behind sunshades which had darkened themselves as much as they could. Finally, we were there. We climbed the last, low hill.

"Behold," said Rameses.

"*¡Madre de Dios!*" said Dos Santos.

Hasan grunted.

Red Wig turned toward me quickly, then turned away. I couldn't read her expression because of the shades. Ellen kept fanning herself.

"What are they doing? asked Myshtigo. It was the first time I had seen him genuinely surprised.

"Why, they're dismantling the great pyramid of Cheops," I said.

After a time Red Wig asked it.

"Why?"

"Well now," I told her, "they're kind of short on building materials hereabouts, the stuff from Old Cairo being radioactive—so they're obtaining it by knocking apart that old piece of solid geometry out there."

"They are desecrating a monument to the past glories of the human race!" she exclaimed.

"Nothing is cheaper than past glories," I observed. "It's the present that we're concerned with, and they need building materials now."

"For how long has this been going on?" asked Myshtigo, his words rushing together.

"It was three days ago," said Rameses, "that we began the dismantling."

"What gives you the right to do a thing like that?"

"It was authorized by the Earthoffice Department of Arts, Monuments and Archives, Srin."

Myshtigo turned to me, his amber eyes glowing strangely.

"You!" he said.

"I," I acknowledged, "am Commissioner thereof—that is correct."

"Why has no one else heard of this action of yours?"

"Because very few people come here anymore," I explained. —"Which is another good reason for dismantling the thing. It doesn't even get looked at much these days. I do have the authority to authorize such actions."

"I came here from another world to see it!"

"Well, take a quick look, then," I told him. "It's going away fast."

He turned and stared.

"You obviously have no conception of its intrinsic value. Or if you do . . ."

"On the contrary, I know exactly what it's worth."

". . . And those unfortunate creatures you have working down there"—his voice rose as he studied the scene —"under the hot rays of your ugly sun—they're laboring under the most primitive conditions! Haven't you ever heard of moving machinery?"

"Of course. It's expensive."

"All those men volunteered for the job, at token salaries—and Actors' Equity won't let us use the whips, even though the men argued in favor of it. All we're allowed to do is crack them in the air near them."

"Actors' Equity?"

"Their union. —Want to see some machinery?" I gestured. "Look up on that hill."

He did.

"What's going on there?"

"We're recording it on viewtape."

"To what end?"

"When we're finished we're going to edit it down to viewable length and run it backwards. 'The Building of the Great Pyramid,' we're going to call it. Should be good for some laughs—also money. Your historians have been conjecturing as to exactly how we put it together ever since the day they heard about it. This may make them somewhat happier. I decided a B.F.M.I. operation would go over best."

"B.F.M.I.?"

"Brute Force and Massive Ignorance. Look at them jamming it up, will you?—following the camera, lying down and standing up quickly when it swings in their direction. They'll be collapsing all over the place in the finished product. But then, this is the first Earthfilm in years. They're real excited."

Dos Santos regarded Red Wig's bared teeth and the bunched muscles beneath her eyes. He glared at the pyramid.

"You are a madman!" he announced.

"No," I replied. "The absence of a monument can, in its own way, be something of a monument also."

"A monument to Conrad Nomikos," he stated.

"No," said Red Wig then. "There is destructive art as surely as there is creative art. I think he may be attempting such a thing. He is playing Caligula. Perhaps I can even see why."

"Thank you."

"You are not welcome. I said 'perhaps.' —An artist does it with love."

"Love is a negative form of hatred."

" 'I am dying, Egypt, dying,' " said Ellen.

Myshtigo laughed.

"You are tougher than I thought, Nomikos," he observed. "But you are not indispensable."

"Try having a civil servant fired—especially me."

"It might be easier than you think."

"We'll see."

"We may."

We turned again toward the great 90 percent

pyramid of Cheops/Khufu. Myshtigo began taking notes once more.

"I'd rather you viewed it from here, for now," I said. "Our presence would waste valuable footage. We're anachronisms. We can go down during coffee break."

"I agree," said Myshtigo, "and I am certain I know an anachronism when I see one. But I have seen all that I care to here. Let us go back to the inn. I wish to talk with the locals."

After a moment, "I'll see Sakkara ahead of schedule, then," he mused. "You haven't begun dismantling all the monuments of Luxor, Karnak, and the Valley of Kings yet, have you?"

"Not yet, no."

"Good. Then we'll visit them ahead of time."

"Then let's not stand here," said Ellen. "This heat is beastly."

So we returned.

"Do you really mean everything you say?" asked Diane as we walked back.

"In my fashion."

"How do you think of such things?"

"In Greek, of course. Then I translate them into English. I'm real good at it."

"Who are you?"

"Ozymandias. Look at my works ye mighty and despair."

"I'm not mighty."

"I wonder. . . ." I said, and I left the part of her face that I could see wearing a rather funny expression as we walked along.

"Let me tell you of the boadile," said I.

Our felucca moved slowly along that dazzling

waterpath that burns its way before the great gray colonnades of Luxor. Myshtigo's back was to me. He was staring at those columns, dictating an occasional impression.

"Where will we put ashore?" he asked me.

"About a mile further up ahead. Perhaps I had better tell you about the boadile."

"I know what a boadile is. I told you that I had studied your world."

"Uh-huh. Reading about them is one thing . . ."

"I have also *seen* boadiles. There are four in the Earthgarden on Taler."

". . . and seeing them in a tank is another thing."

"Between yourself and Hasan we are a veritable floating aresenal. I count three grenades on your belt, four on his."

"You can't use a grenade if one is on top of you —not without defeating the purpose of self-defense, that is. If it's any further away you can't hit it with one. They move too fast."

He finally turned.

"What *do* you use?"

I reached inside my galabieh (having gone native) and withdrew the weapon I always try to have on hand when I come this way.

He examined it.

"Name it."

"It's a machine-pistol. Fires meta-cyanide slugs —one ton impact when a round strikes. Not real accurate, but that's not necessary. It's patterned after a twentieth century handgun called a Schmeisser."

"It's rather unwieldy. Will it stop a boadile?"

"If you're lucky. I have a couple more in one of the cases. Want one?"

"No, thank you." He paused. "But you can tell me more about the boadile. I really only glanced at them that day, and they were pretty well submerged."

"Well . . . Head something like a croc's, only bigger. Around forty feet long. Able to roll itself into a big beachball with teeth. Fast on land or in water—and a hell of a lot of little legs on each side—"

"How many legs?" he interrupted.

"Hm." I stopped. "To tell you absolute truth, I've never counted. Just a second.

"Hey, George," I called out, to where Earth's eminent chief biologist lay dozing in the shade of the sail. "How many legs on a boadile?"

He rose to his feet, stretched slightly and came up beside us.

"Boadiles," he mused, poking a finger into his ear and leafing through the files inside. "They're definitely of the class reptilia—of that much we're certain. Whether they're of the order crocodilia, suborder of their own, or whether they're of the order squamata, suborder lacertilia, family neopoda—as a colleague of mine on Taler half-seriously insists—we are not certain. To me they are somewhat reminiscent of pre-Three Day photo-reproduction of artists' conceptions of the Mesozoic phytosaurus with, of course, the supernumerary legs and the constrictive ability. So I favor the order crocodilia myself."

He leaned on the rail and stared out across the shimmering water.

I saw then that he wasn't about to say anything else, so, "So how many legs on one?" I asked again.

"Eh? Legs? I never counted them. If we're lucky we might get a chance to, though. There are lots around here. —The young one I had didn't last too long."

"What happened to it?" asked Myshtigo.

"My megadonaplaty ate it."

"Megadonaplaty?"

"Sort of like a duck-billed platypus with teeth," I explained, "and about ten feet high. Picture that. So far as we know, they've only been seen about three or four times. Australian. We got ours through a fortunate accident. Probably won't last, as a species—the way boadiles will, I mean. They're oviparous mammals, and their eggs are too large for a hungry world to permit the continuance of the species—if it is a true species. Maybe they're just isolated sports."

"Perhaps," said George, nodding wisely; "and then again perhaps not."

Myshtigo turned away, shaking his head.

Hasan had partly unpacked his robot golem—Rolem—and was fooling with its controls. Ellen had finally given up on simicoloring and was lying in the sun getting burnt all over. Red Wig and Dos Santos were plotting something at the other end of the vessel. Those two never just meet; they always have assignations. Our felucca moved slowly along the dazzling waterpath that burns its way before the great gray colonnades of Luxor, and I decided it was time to head it in toward the shore and see what was new among the tombs and ruined temples.

The next six days were rather uneventful and somewhat unforgettable, extremely active, and sort of ugly-beautiful—in the way that a flower can be, with its petals all intact and a dark and runny rot-spot in the center. Here's how. . . .

Myshtigo must have interviewed every stone ram along the four miles of the Way to Karnak. Both in the blaze of day and by torchlight we navigated the ruins, disturbing bats, rats, snakes and insects, listening to the Vegan's monotonous note-taking in his monotonous language. At night we camped on the sands, setting up a two hundred meter electrical warning perimeter and posting two guards. The boadile is cold-blooded; the nights were chill. So there was relatively little danger from without.

Huge campfires lighted the nights, all about the areas we chose, because the Vegan wanted things primitive—for purposes of atmosphere, I guessed. Our Skimmers were further south. We had flown them to a place I knew of and left them there under Office guard, renting the felucca for our trip—which paralleled the King-God's journey from Karnak to Luxor. Myshtigo had wanted it that way. Nights, Hasan would either practice with the *assagai* he had bartered from a big Nubian, or he would strip to the waist and wrestle for hours with his tireless golem.

A worthy opponent was the golem. Hasan had it programmed at twice the statistically-averaged strength of a man and had upped its reflex-time by fifty percent. Its "memory" contained hundreds of wrestling holds, and its governor theoretically prevented it from killing or maiming its opponent—all through a series of chemelectrical afferent nerve-analogues which permitted it to gauge to an ounce the amount of pressure necessary to snap a bone or tear a tendon. Rolem was about five feet, six inches in height and weighed around two hundred fifty pounds; manufactured on Bakab, he was quite expensive, was dough-colored and caricature-featured, and his brains were located somewhere below where his navel would be—if golems had navels—to protect his think stuff from Greco-Roman shocks. Even as it is, accidents can happen. People have been killed by the things, when something goes amok in the brains or some afferents, or just because the people themselves slipped or tried to jerk away, supplying the necessary extra ounces. I'd had one once, for almost a year, programmed for boxing. I used to spend fifteen minutes or so with it every afternoon. Got to thinking of it as a person, almost. Then one day it fouled me and I pounded it for over an hour and finally knocked its head off. The thing kept right on boxing, and I stopped thinking of it as a friendly sparring partner right then. It's a weird feeling, boxing with a headless golem, you know? Sort of like waking from a pleasant dream and finding a nightmare crouched at the foot of your bed. It doesn't really "see" its opponent with those eye-things it has; it's all sheathed about with piezo-electric radar mesentery, and it "watches" from all its surfaces. Still, the death of an illusion tends to disconcert. I turned mine off and never turned it back on again. Sold it to a camel trader for a pretty good price. Don't know if he ever got the head back on. But he was a Turk, so who cares?

Anyway—Hasan would tangle with Rolem, both of them gleaming in the firelight, and we'd all sit on blankets and watch, and bats would swoop low occasionally, like big, fast ashes, and emaciated clouds would cover the moon, veil-like, and then move on again. It was that way on the third night, when I went mad.

I remember it only in the way you remember a passing countryside you might have seen through a late summer evening storm—as a series of isolated, lightning-filled stillshots. . . .

Having spoken with Cassandra for the better part of an hour, I concluded the transmission with a promise to cop a Skimmer the following afternoon and spend the next night on Kos. I recall our last words.

"Take care, Konstantin. I have been dreaming bad dreams."

"Bosh, Cassandra. Good night."

And who knows but that her dreams might have been the result of a temporal shockwave moving backwards from a 9.6 Richter reading?

A certain cruel gleam filling his eyes, Dos Santos applauded as Hasan hurled Rolem to the ground with a thunderous crash. That particular earthshaker continued, however, long after the golem had climbed back to his feet and gotten into another crouch, his arms doing serpent-things in the Arab's direction. The ground shook and shook.

"What power! Still do I feel it!" cried Dos Santos. "Olé!"

"It is a seismic disturbance," said George. "Even though I'm not a geologist—"

"Earthquake!" yelled his wife, dropping an unpasturized date she had been feeding Myshtigo.

There was no reason to run, no place to run to. There was nothing nearby that could fall on us. The ground was level and pretty barren. So we just sat there and were thrown about, even knocked flat a few times. The fires did amazing things.

Rolem's time was up and he went stiff then, and Hasan came and sat with George and me. The tremors lasted the better part of an hour, and they came again, more weakly, many times during that night. After the first bad shock had run its course, we got in touch with the Port. The instruments there showed that the center of the thing lay a good distance to the north of us.

A bad distance, really.

. . . In the Mediterranean.

The Aegean, to be more specific.

I felt sick, and suddenly I was.

I tried to put through a call to Kos.

Nothing.

My Cassandra, my lovely lady, my princess. . . . Where was she? For two hours I tried to find out. Then the Port called me.

It was Lorel's voice, not just some lob watch operator's.

"Uh—Conrad, I don't know how to tell you, exactly, what happened . . ."

"Just talk," I said, "and stop when you're finished."

"An observe-satellite passed your way about twelve minutes ago," he crackled across the bands. "Several of the Aegean islands were no longer present in the pictures it transmitted . . ."

"No," I said.

"I'm afraid that Kos was one of them."

"No," I said.

"I'm sorry," he told me, "but that is the way it shows. I don't know what else to say. . . ."

"That's enough," I said. "That's all. That's it. Goodbye. We'll talk more later. No! I guess—No!"

"Wait! Conrad!"

I went mad.

Bats, shaken loose from the night, were swooping

about me. I struck out with my right hand and killed one as it flashed in my direction. I waited a few seconds and killed another. Then I picked up a big rock with both hands and was about to smash the radio when George laid a hand on my shoulder, and I dropped the rock and knocked his hand away and backhanded him across the mouth. I don't know what became of him then, but as I stooped to raise the rock once more I heard the sound of footfalls behind me. I dropped to one knee and pivoted on it, scooping up a handful of sand to throw in someone's eyes. They were all of them there: Myshtigo and Red Wig and Dos Santos, Rameses, Ellen, three local civil servants, and Hasan—approaching in a group. Someone yelled "Scatter!" when they saw my face, and they fanned out.

Then they were everyone I'd ever hated—I could feel it. I saw other faces, heard other voices. Everyone I'd ever known, hated, wanted to smash, had smashed, stood there resurrected before the fire, and only the whites of their teeth were showing through the shadows that crossed over their faces as they smiled and came toward me, bearing various dooms in their hands, and soft, persuasive words on their lips—so I threw the sand at the foremost and rushed him.

My uppercut knocked him over backward, then two Egyptians were on me from both sides.

I shook them loose, and in the corner of my colder eye saw a great Arab with something like a black avocado in his hand. He was swinging it toward my head, so I dropped down. He had been coming in my direction and I managed to give his stomach more than just a shove, so he sat down suddenly. Then the two men I had thrown away were back on me again. A woman was screaming, somewhere in the distance, but I couldn't see any women.

I tore my right arm free and batted someone with it, and the man went down and another took his place. From straight ahead a blue man threw a rock which struck me on the shoulder and only made me madder. I raised a kicking body into the air and threw it against another, then I hit someone with my fist. I shook myself. My galabieh was torn and dirty, so I tore it the rest of the way off and threw it away.

I looked around. They had stopped coming at me, and it wasn't fair—it wasn't fair that they should stop then when I wanted so badly to see things breaking. So I raised up the man at my feet and slapped him down again. Then I raised him up again and someone yelled "Eh! Karaghiosis!" and began calling me names in broken Greek. I let the man fall back to the ground and turned.

There, before the fire—there were two of them: one tall and bearded, the other squat and heavy and hairless and molded out of a mixture of putty and earth.

"My friend says he will break you, Greek!" called out the tall one, as he did something to the other's back.

I moved toward them and the man of putty and mud sprang at me.

He tripped me, but I came up again fast and caught him beneath the armpits and threw him off to the side. But he recovered his footing as rapidly as I had, and he came back again and caught me behind the neck with one hand. I did the same to him, also seizing his elbow—and we locked together there, and he was strong.

Because he was strong, I kept changing holds, testing his strength. He was also fast, accommodating every move I made almost as soon as I thought of it.

I threw my arms up between his, hard, and stepped back on my reinforced leg. Freed for a moment, we orbited each other, seeking another opening.

I kept my arms low and I was bent well forward because of his shortness. For a moment my arms were too near my sides, and he moved in faster than I had seen anyone move before, ever, and he caught me in a body lock that squeezed the big flat flowers of moisture out of my pores and caused a great pain in my sides.

Still his arms tightened, and I knew that it would not be long before he broke me unless I could break his hold.

I doubled my hands into fists and got them against his belly and pushed. His grip tightened. I stepped backward and heaved forward with both arms. My hands went up higher between us and I got my right fist against the palm of my left hand and began to push them together and lift with my arms. My head swam as my arms came up higher, and my kidneys were on fire. Then I tightened all the muscles in my back and my shoulders and felt the strength flow down through my arms and come together in my hands, and I smashed them up toward the sky and his chin happened to be in the way, but it didn't stop them.

My arms shot up over my head and he fell backward.

It should have broken a man's neck, the force of

that big snap that came when my hands struck his chin and he got a look at his heels from the backside.

But he sprang up immediately, and I knew then that he was no mortal wrestler, but one of those creatures born not of woman; rather, I knew, he had been torn Antaeus-like from the womb of the Earth herself.

I brought my hands down hard on his shoulders and he dropped to his knees. I caught him across the throat then and stepped to his right side and got my left knee under the lower part of his back. I leaned forward, bearing down on his thighs and shoulders, trying to break him.

But I couldn't. He just kept bending until his head touched the ground and I couldn't push him any further.

No one's back bends like that and doesn't snap, but his did.

Then I heaved up with my knee and let go, and he was on me again—that fast.

So I tried to strangle him. My arms were much longer than his. I caught him by the throat with both hands, my thumbs pressing hard against what should have been his windpipe. He got his arms across mine though, at the elbows and inside, and began to pull downward and out. I kept squeezing, waiting for his face to darken, his eyes to bug out. My elbows began to bend under his downward pressure.

Then his arms came across and caught me by the throat.

And we stood there and choked one another. Only he wouldn't be strangled.

His thumbs were like two spikes pressing into the

muscles in my neck. I felt my face flush. My temples began to throb.

Off in the distance, I heard a scream:

"Stop it, Hasan! It's not supposed to do that!"

It sounded like Red Wig's voice. Anyhow, that's the name that came into my head: Red Wig. Which meant that Donald Dos Santos was somewhere nearby. And she had said "Hasan," a name written on another picture that came suddenly clear.

Which meant that I was Conrad and that I was in Egypt, and that the expressionless face swimming before me was therefore that of the golem-wrestler, Rolem, a creature which could be set for five times the strength of a human being and probably was so set, a creature which could be given the reflexes of an adrenalized cat, and doubtless had them in full operation.

Only a golem wasn't supposed to kill, except by accident, and Rolem was trying to kill me.

Which meant that his governor wasn't functioning.

I released my choke, seeing that it wasn't working, and I placed the palm of my left hand beneath his right elbow. Then I reached across the top of his arms and seized his right wrist with my other hand, and I crouched as low as I could and pushed up on his elbow and pulled up on his wrist.

As he went off balance to his left and the grip was broken I kept hold of the wrist, twisting it so that the elbow was exposed upwards. I stiffened my left hand, snapped it up beside my ear, and brought it down across the elbow joint.

Nothing. There was no snapping sound. The arm just gave way, bending backward at an unnatural angle.

I released the wrist and he fell to one knee. Then he stood again, quickly, and as he did so the arm straightened itself and then bent forward again into a normal position.

If I knew Hasan's mind, then Rolem's timer had been set for maximum—two hours. Which was a pretty long time, all things considered.

But this time around I knew who I was and what I was doing. Also, I knew what went into the structuring of a golem. This one was a wrestling golem. Therefore, it could not box.

I cast a quick look back over my shoulder, to the place where I had been standing when the whole thing had started—over by the radio tent. It was about fifty feet away.

He almost had me then. Just during that split second while I had turned my attention to the rear he had reached out and seized me behind the neck with one hand and caught me beneath the chin with the other.

He might have broken my neck, had he been able to follow through, but there came another tremblor at that moment—a severe one, which cast us both to the ground—and I broke this hold, also.

I scrambled to my feet seconds later, and the earth was still shaking. Rolem was up too, though, and facing me again.

We were like two drunken sailors fighting on a storm-tossed ship. . . .

He came at me and I gave ground.

I hit him with a left jab, and while he snatched at my arm I punched him in the stomach. Then I backed off.

He came on again and I kept throwing punches. Boxing was to him what the fourth dimension is to me—he just couldn't see it. He kept advancing, shaking off my punches, and I kept retreating in the direction of the radio tent, and the ground kept shaking, and somewhere a woman was screaming, and I heard a shouted "Olé!" as I landed a right below the belt, hoping to jar his brains a bit.

Then we were there and I saw what I wanted—the big rock I'd intended to use on the radio. I feinted with my left, then seized him, shoulder-and-thigh, and raised him high up over my head.

I bent backwards, tightened up my muscles, and hurled him down upon the rock.

It caught him in the stomach.

He began to rise again, but more slowly than he had before, and I kicked him in the stomach three times, with my great reinforced right boot, and I watched him sink back down.

A strange whirring sound had begun in his mid-section.

The ground shook again. Rolem crumpled, stretched out, and the only sign of motion was in the fingers of his left hand. They kept clenching and unclenching—reminding me, oddly, of Hasan's hands that night back at the *hounfor*.

Then I turned slowly and they were all standing there: Myshtigo and Ellen, and Dos Santos with a puffed-up cheek, Red Wig, George, Rameses and Hasan, and the three plastaged Egyptians. I took a step toward them then and they began to fan out again, their faces filling with fear. But I shook my head.

"No, I'm all right now," I said, "but leave me alone. I'm going down to the river to bathe." I took seven steps, and then someone must have pulled out the plug, because I gurgled, everything swirled, and the world ran away down the drain.

The days that followed were ashes and the nights were iron. The spirit that had been torn from my soul was buried deeper than any mummy that lay mouldering beneath those sands. It is said that the dead forget the dead in the house of Hades, Cassandra, but I hoped it was not so. I went through the motions of conducting a tour, and Lorel suggested that I appoint someone else to finish it out and take a leave of absence myself.

I couldn't.

What would I do then? Sit and brood in some Old Place, cadging drinks from unwary travelers? No. Some kind of motion is always essential at such times; its forms eventually generate a content for their empty insides. So I went on with the tour and turned my attention to the small mysteries it contained.

I took Rolem apart and studied his governor. It *had* been broken, of course—which meant that either I had done it during the early stages of our conflict, or Hasan had done it as he had souped him up to take the fight out of me. If Hasan had done it, then he did not just want me beaten, but dead. If such was the case, then the question was, *Why?* I wondered whether his employer knew that I had once been Karaghiosis. If he did, though, why should he want to kill the founder and first Secretary of his own Party?—the man who had sworn that he would not see the Earth sold out from under him and turned into a sporting house by a pack of blue aliens—not see it without fighting, anyhow—and had organized about himself a cabal which systematically lowered the value of all Vegan-owned Terran property to zero, and even went so far as to raze the Talerites' lush realty office on Madagascar —the man whose ideals he allegedly espoused, though they were currently being channeled into more peaceful, legalistic modes of property-defense —why should he want *that* man dead?

There, he had either sold out the Party, or he didn't know who I was and had had some other end in mind when he'd instructed Hasan to kill me.

Or else Hasan was acting under someone else's orders.

But who else could there be? And again, why?

I had no answer. I decided I wanted one.

The first condolence had been George's.

"I'm sorry, Conrad," he'd said, looking past my elbow, and then down at the sand, and then glancing up quickly into my face.

Saying human things upset him, and made him want to go away. I could tell. It is doubtful that the parade consisting of Ellen and myself, which had passed that previous summer, had occupied much of his attention. His passions stopped outside the biological laboratory. I remember when he'd dissected the last dog on Earth. After four years of scratching his ears and combing the fleas from his tail and listening to him bark, George had called Rolf to him one day. Rolf had trotted in, bringing along the old dishrag they'd always played at tug-of-war with, and George had tugged him real close and give him a hypo and then opened him up. He'd wanted to get him while he was still in his prime. Still has the skeleton mounted in his lab. He'd also wanted to raise his kids—Mark and Dorothy and Jim—in Skinner Boxes, but Ellen had put her foot down each time (like *bang! bang! bang!*) in postpregnancy seizures of motherhood which had lasted for at least a month—which had been just long enough to spoil the initial stimuli-balances George had wanted to establish. So I couldn't really see him as having much desire to take my measure for a wooden sleeping bag of the underground sort. If he'd wanted me dead, it would probably have been subtle, fast, and exotic—with something like Divban rabbit-venom. But no, he didn't care that much. I was sure.

Ellen herself, while she is capable of intense feelings, is ever the faulty windup doll. Something always goes *sprong* before she can take action on her feelings, and by the next day she feels as strongly about something else. She'd choked me to death back at the Port, and as far as she was concerned that affair was a dead issue. Her condolence went something like this:

"Conrad, you just don't know how sorry I am! *Really*. Even though I never met her, I *know* how you must feel," and her voice went up and down the scale, and I knew she believed what she was saying, and I thanked her too.

Hasan, though, came up beside me while I was standing there, staring out over the suddenly swollen and muddy Nile. We stood together for a time and then he said, "Your woman is gone and your heart is heavy. Words will not lighten the weight, and what is written is written. But let it also be put down that I grieve with you." Then we stood there awhile longer and he walked away.

I didn't wonder about him. He was the one person who could be dismissed, even though his hand had set the machine in motion. He never held grudges; he never killed for free. He had no personal motive to kill me. That his condolences were genuine, I was certain. Killing me would have nothing to do with the sincerity of his feelings in a matter like this. A true professional must respect some sort of boundary between self and task.

Myshtigo said no words of sympathy. It would have been alien to his nature. Among the Vegans, death is a time of rejoicing. On the spiritual level it means *sagl*—completion—the fragmentation of the psyche into little pleasure-sensing pinpricks, which are scattered all over the place to participate in the great universal orgasm; and on the material plane it is represented by *ansakundabad't*—the ceremonial auditing of most of the deceased's personal possessions, the reading of his distribution-desire and the division of his wealth, accompanied by much feasting, singing, and drinking.

Dos Santos said to me: "It is a sad thing that has happened to you, my friend. It is to lose the blood of one's own veins to lose one's woman. Your sorrow is great and you cannot be comforted. It is like a smoldering fire that will not die out, and it is a sad and terrible thing.

"Death is cruel and it is dark," he finished, and his eyes were moist—for be it Gypsy, Jew, Moor, or what have you, a victim is a victim to a Spaniard, a thing to be appreciated on one of those mystically obscure levels which I lack.

Then Red Wig came up beside me and said, "Dreadful. . . . Sorry. Nothing else to say, to do, but sorry."

I nodded.

"Thanks."

"And there is something I must ask you. Not now, though. Later."

"Sure," I said, and I returned to watching the river after they left, and I thought about those last two. They had sounded as sorry as everyone else, but it seemed they had to be mixed up in the golem business, somehow. I was sure, though, that it had been Diane who had screamed while Rolem had been choking me, screamed for Hasan to stop him. That left Don, and I had by then come to entertain strong doubts that he ever did anything without first consulting her.

Which left nobody.

And there was no real motive apparent. . . .

And it could all have been an accident. . . .

But . . .

But I had this feeling that someone wanted to kill me. I knew that Hasan was not above taking two jobs at the same time, and for different employers, if there was no conflict of interests.

And this made me happy.

It gave me a purpose, something to do.

There's really nothing quite like someone's wanting you dead to make you want to go on living. I would find him, find out why, and stop him.

Death's second pass was fast, and as much as I would have liked to have pinned it on human agent, I couldn't. It was just one of those diddles of dumb destiny which sometimes come like uninvited guests at dinnertime. Its finale, however, left me quite puzzled and gave me some new, confusing thoughts to think.

It came like this. . . .

Down by the river, that great fertile flooder, that eraser of boundaries and father of plane geometry, sat the Vegan, making sketches of the opposite bank. I suppose had he been on *that* bank he would have been sketching the one he sat upon, but this is cynical conjecture. What bothered me was the fact that he had come off alone, down to this warm, marshy spot, had not told anyone where he was going, and had brought along nothing more lethal than a No. 2 pencil.

It happened.

An old, mottled log which had been drifting in near the shore suddenly ceased being an old, mottled log. A long, serpentine back end whipped skyward, a bushel full of teeth appeared at the other end, and lots of little legs found solid ground and stared acting like wheels.

I yelled and snatched at my belt.

Myshtigo dropped his pad and bolted.

It was on him, though, and I couldn't fire then.

So I made a dash, but by the time I got there it had two coils around him and he was about two shades bluer, and those teeth were closing in on him.

Now, there is one way to make any kind of constrictor loosen up, at least for a moment. I grabbed for its high head, which had slowed down just a bit as it contemplated its breakfast, and I managed to catch my fingers under the scaly ridges at the sides of that head.

I dug my thumbs into its eyes as hard as I could.

Then a spastic giant hit me with a graygreen ship.

I picked myself up and I was about ten feet from where I had been standing. Myshtigo had been thrown further up the bank. He was recovering his feet just as it attacked again.

Only it attacked me, not him.

It reared up about eight feet off the ground and toppled toward me. I threw myself to the side and that big, flat head missed me by inches, its impact showering me with dirt and pebbles.

I rolled further and started to rise, but the tail came around and knocked me down again. Then I scrambled backward, but was too late to avoid the coil it threw. It caught me low around the hips and I fell again.

Then a pair of blue arms wrapped themselves around the body above the coil, but they couldn't hold on for more than a few seconds. Then we were both tied up in knots.

I struggled, but how do you fight a thick, slippery armored cable with messes of little legs that keep tearing at you? My right arm was pinned to my side by then, and I couldn't reach far enough with my left hand to do any more gouging. The coils tightened. The head moved toward me and I tore at the body. I beat at it and I clawed it, and I finally managed to tear my right arm free, giving up some skin in the process.

I blocked with my right hand as the head descended. My hand came up beneath the lower jaw, caught it, and held it there, keeping the head back. The big coil tightened around my waist, more powerful than even the grip of the golem had been. Then it shook its head sideways, away from my hand, and the head came down and the jaws opened wide.

Myshtigo's struggles must have irritated it and slowed it some, giving me time for my last defense.

I thrust my hands up into its mouth and held its jaws apart.

The roof of its mouth was slimy and my palm

began to slip along it, slowly. I pressed down harder on the lower jaw, as hard as I could. The mouth opened another half foot and seemed locked there.

It tried to draw back then, to make me let go, but its coils bound us too tightly to give it the necessary footage.

So it unwound a little, straightening some, and pulling back its head. I gained a kneeling position. Myshtigo was in a sagging crouch about six feet away from me.

My right hand slipped some more, almost to the point where I would lose all my leverage.

Then I heard a great cry.

The shudder came almost simultaneously. I snapped my arms free as I felt the thing's strength wane for a second. There was a dreadful clicking of teeth and a final constriction. I blacked out for a moment.

Then I was fighting free, untangling myself. The smooth wooden shaft which had skewered the boadile was taking the life from it, and its movements suddenly became spasmodic rather than aggressive.

I was knocked down twice by all its lashing about, but I got Myshtigo free, and we got about fifty feet away and watched it die. This took quite awhile.

Hasan stood there, expressionless. The assagai he had spent so much time practicing with had done its work. When George dissected the creature later we learned that the shaft had lodged within two inches of its heart, severing the big artery. By the way, it had two dozen legs, evenly distributed on either side, as might be expected.

Dos Santos stood beside Hasan and Diane stood

beside Dos Santos. Everyone else from the camp was there, too.

"Good show," I said. "Fine shot. Thanks."

"It was nothing," Hasan replied.

It was nothing, he had said. Nothing but the death blow to my motion that he had gimmicked the golem. If Hasan had tried to kill me then, why should he have saved me from the boadile?

Unless what he had said back at the Port was the overriding truth—that he *had* been hired to protect the Vegan. If that was his main job and killing me was only secondary, then he would have had to save me as a by-product of keeping Myshtigo alive.

But then . . .

Oh hell. Forget it.

I threw a stone as far as I could, and another. Our Skimmer would be flown up to our campsite the following day and we would take off for Athens, stopping only to drop Rameses and the three others at New Cairo. I was glad I was leaving Egypt, with its must and its dust and its dead, half-animal deities. I was already sick of the place.

Then Phil's call came through from the Port, and Rameses called me into the radio tent.

"Yeah?" said I, to the radio.

"Conrad, this is Phil. I've just written her elegy and I should like to read it to you. Even though I never met her, I've heard you speak of her and I've seen her picture, so I think I've done a pretty good job—"

"Please, Phil. I'm not interested in the consolations of poetry right now. Some other time, perhaps—"

"This is not one of the fill-in sort. I know that you

do not like those, and in a way I do not blame you."

My hand hovered above the cutoff toggle, paused, reached for one of Ramses' cigarettes instead.

"Sure, go ahead. I'm listening."

And he did, and it wasn't a bad job, either. I don't remember much of it. I just remember those crisp, clear words coming from halfway around the world, and me standing there, bruised inside and out, hearing them. He described the virtues of the Nymph whom Poseidon had reached for but lost to his brother Hades. He called for a general mourning among the elements. And as he spoke my mind went time-traveling back to those two happy months on Kos, and everything since then was erased; and we were back aboard the *Vanitie,* sailing toward our picnic islet with its semi-sacred grove, and we were bathing together, and lying together in the sun, holding hands and not saying anything, just feeling the sunfall, like a waterfall bright and dry and gentle, come down upon our pink and naked spirits, there on the endless beach that circled and circled the tiny realm and always came back to us.

And he was finished and cleared his throat a couple times, and my isle sank from sight, carrying that one part of me along with it, because that was the time that was.

"Thanks, Phil," I said. "That was very nice."

"I am pleased that you find it appropriate," he said. Then, "I am flying to Athens this afternoon. I should like to join you on this leg of your tour, if it is all right with you."

"Surely," I replied. "May I ask why, though?"

"I have decided that I want to see Greece once

more. Since you are going to be there it might make it seem a little more like the old days. I'd like to take a last look at some of the Old Places."

"You make it sound rather final."

"Well . . . I've pushed the S-S series about as far as it will go. I fancy I can feel the mainspring running down now. Maybe it will take a few more windings and maybe it won't. At any rate, I want to see Greece again and I feel as if this is my last chance."

"I'm sure you're wrong, but we'll all be dining at the Garden Altar tomorrow evening, around eight."

"Fine. I'll see you then."

"Check."

"Goodbye, Conrad."

"Goodbye."

I went and showered and rubbed me with liniment, and I put on clean clothing. I was still sore in several places, but at least I felt clean. Then I went and found the Vegan, who had just finished doing the same thing, and I fixed him with my baleful glare.

"Correct me if I'm wrong," I stated, "but one of the reasons you wanted me to run this show is because I have a high survival potential. Is that correct?"

"That is correct."

"Thus far, I have done my best to see that it did not remain potential, but that it was actively employed to promote the general welfare."

"Was that what you were doing when you attacked the entire group single-handed?"

I started to reach for his throat, thought better of it, dropped my hand. I was rewarded by a flicker of fear that widened his eyes and twitched the corners of his mouth. He took a step backward.

"I'll overlook that," I told him. "I am here only to take you where you want to go, and to see that you come back with a whole skin. You caused me a small problem this morning by making yourself available as boadile bait. Be warned, therefore, that one does not go to hell to light a cigarette. Whether you wish to go off by yourself, check first to see whether you are in safe country." His gaze faltered. He looked away. "If you are not," I continued, "then take along an armed escort—since you refuse to carry weapons yourself. That is all I have to say. If you do not wish to cooperate, tell me now and I'll quit and get you another guide. Lorel has already suggested that I do this, anyhow.

"So what's the word?" I asked.

"Did Lorel really say that?"

"Yes."

"How extraordinary. . . . Well, certainly, yes. I shall comply with your request. I see that it is a prudent one."

"Great. You said you want to visit the Valley of Queens again this afternoon. Rameses will take you. I don't feel like doing it myself. We're pulling out tomorrow morning at ten. Be ready."

I walked away then, waiting for him to say something—just one word even.

He didn't.

Fortunately, both for the survivors and for the generations as yet unborn, Scotland had not been hard hit during the Three Days. I fetched a bucket of ice from the freeze-unit and a bottle of soda from our mess tent. I turned on the cooling coil beside my bunk, opened a fifth from out of my private stock, and spent the rest of the afternoon reflecting upon the futility of all human endeavor.

Late that evening, after I had sobered up to an acceptable point and scrounged me a bite to eat, I armed myself and went looking for some fresh air.

I heard voices as I neared the eastern end of the warning perimeter, so I sat down in darkness, resting my back against a largish rock, and tried to eavesdrop. I'd recognized the vibrant diminuendoes of Myshtigo's voice, and I wanted to hear what he was saying.

I couldn't, though.

They were a little too far away, and desert acoustics are not always the finest in the world. I sat there straining with that part of me which listens, and it happened as it sometimes does:

I was seated on a blanket beside Ellen and my arm was around her shoulders. My blue arm. . . .

The whole thing faded as I recoiled from the notion of being a Vegan, even in a pseudotelepathic wish-fulfillment, and I was back beside my rock once again.

I was lonesome, though, and Ellen had seemed softer than the rock, and I was still curious.

So I found myself back there once more, observing. . . .

". . . can't see it from here," I was saying, "but Vega is a star of the first magnitude, located in what your people call the constellation Lyra."

"What's it like on Taler?" asked Ellen.

There was a long pause. Then:

"Meaningful things are often the things people are least able to describe. Sometimes, though, it is a problem in communicating something for which there is no corresponding element in the person to whom you are speaking. Taler is not like this place. There are no deserts. The entire world is landscaped. But . . . Let me take that flower from your hair. There. Look at it. What do you see?"

"A pretty white flower. That's why I picked it and put it in my hair."

"But it is *not* a pretty white flower. Not to me, anyhow. Your *eyes* perceive light with wavelengths between about 4000 and 7200 angstrom units. The eyes of a Vegan look deeper into the ultraviolet, for one thing, down to around 3000. We are blind to what you refer to as 'red,' but on this 'white' flower I see two colors for which there are no words in your language. My body is covered with patterns you cannot see, but they are close enough to those of the others in my family so that another Vegan, familiar with the Shtigogens, could tell my family and province on our first meeting. Some of our paintings look garish to Earth eyes, or even seem to be all of one color—blue, usually—because the subtleties are invisible to them. Much of our music would seem to you to contain big gaps of silence, gaps which are actually filled with melody. Our cities are clean and logically disposed. They catch the light of day and hold it long into the night. They are places of slow movement, pleasant sounds. This means much to me, but I do not know how to describe it to a—human."

"But people—Earth people, I mean—live on your worlds. . . ."

"But they do not really see them or hear them or feel them the way we do. There is a gulf we can appreciate and understand, but we cannot really cross it. That is why I cannot tell you what Taler is like. It would be a different world to you than the world it is to me."

"I'd like to see it, though. Very much. I think I'd even like to live there."

"I do not believe you would be happy there."

"Why not?"

"Because non-Vegan immigrants are non-Vegan immigrants. You are not of a low caste here. I know you do not use that term, but that is what it amounts to. Your Office personnel and their families are the highest caste on this planet. Wealthy non-Office persons come next, then those who work for the wealthy non-Office persons, followed by those who make their own living from the land; then, at the bottom, are those unfortunates who inhabit the Old Places. You are at the top here. On Taler you would be at the bottom."

"Why must it be that way?" she asked.

"Because you see a white flower." I handed it back.

There was a long silence and a cool breeze.

"Anyhow I'm happy you came here," she said.

"It *is* an interesting place."

"Glad you like it."

"Was the man called Conrad really your lover?"

I recoiled at the suddenness of the question.

"It's none of your blue business," she said, "but the answer is yes."

"I can see why," he said, and I felt uncomfortable and maybe something like a voyeur, or—subtlety of subtleties—one who watches a voyeur watching.

"Why?" she asked.

"Because you want the strange, the powerful, the exotic; because you are never happy being where you are, what you are."

"That's not true. . . . Maybe it is. Yes, he once said something like that to me. Perhaps it is true."

I felt very sorry for her at that moment. Then, without realizing it, as I wanted to console her in some way, I reached out and took her hand. Only it was Myshtigo's hand that moved, and he had not willed it to move. I had.

I was afraid suddenly. So was he, though. I could feel it.

There was a great drunk-like, room-swimming feeling, as I felt that he felt *occupied,* as if he had had sensed another presence within his mind.

I wanted away quickly then, and I was back there beside my rock, but not before she'd dropped the flower and I heard her say, "Hold me!"

Damn those pseudotelepathic wish-fulfillments! I thought. *Someday I'll stop believing that that's all they are.*

I *had* seen two colors in that flower, colors for which I have no words. . . .

I walked back toward the camp. I passed through the camp and kept on going. I reached the other end of the warning perimeter, sat down on the ground, lit a cigarette. The night was cool, the night was dark.

Two cigarettes later I heard a voice behind me, but I did not turn.

"'In the Great House and in the House of Fire, on that Great Day when all the days and years are numbered, oh let my name be given back to me,'" it said.

"Good for you," I said softly. "Appropriate quote. I recognize the Book of the Dead when I hear it taken in vain."

"I wasn't taking it in vain, just—as you said—appropriately."

"Good for you."

"*On* that great day when all the days and years are numbered, if they do give you back your name, then what name will it be?"

"They won't. I plan on being late. And what's in a name, anyhow?"

"Depends on the name. So try 'Karaghiosis.'"

"Try sitting down where I can see you. I don't like to have people standing behind me."

"All right—there. So?"

"So what?"

"So try 'Karaghiosis.'"

"Why should I?"

"Because it means something. At least, it did once."

"Karaghiosis was a figure in the old Greek shadow shows, sort of like Punch in the European Punch and Judy plays. He was a slob and a buffoon."

"He was Greek, and he was subtle."

"Ha! He was half-coward, and he was greasy."

"He was also half-hero. Cunning. Somewhat gross. Sense of humor. *He'd* tear down a pyramid. Also, he was strong, when he wanted to be."

"Where is he now?"

"I'd like to know."

"Why ask me?"

"Because that is the name Hasan called you on the night you fought the golem."

"Oh . . . I see. Well, it was just an expletive, a generic term, a synonym for fool, a nickname—like if I were to call you 'Red.'—And now that I think of it, I wonder how you look to Myshtigo, anyhow? Vegans are blind to the color of your hair, you know?"

"I don't really care how I look to Vegans. Wonder how you look, though. I understand that Myshtigo's file on you is quite thick. Says something about you being several centuries old."

"Doubtless an exaggeration. But you seem to know a lot about it. How thick is your file on Myshtigo?"

"Not very, not yet."

"It seems that you hate him more than you hate everyone else. Is that true?"

"Yes."

"Why?"

"He's a Vegan."

"So?"

"I hate Vegans, is all."

"No, there's more."

"True.—You're quite strong, you know?"

"I know."

"In fact, you're the strongest human being I've ever seen. Strong enough to break the neck of a spiderbat, then fall into the bay at Piraeus and swim ashore and have breakfast."

"Odd example you've chosen."

"Not so, not really. *Did* you?"

"Why?"

"I want to know, need to know."

"Sorry."

"Sorry is not good enough. Talk more."

"Said all."

"No. We need Karaghiosis."

"Who's 'we?'"

"The Radpol. Me."

"Why, again?"

"Hasan is half as old as Time. Karaghiosis is older. Hasan knew him, remembered, called you 'Karaghiosis.' You *are* Karaghiosis, the killer, the defender of Earth—and we need you now. Very badly. Armageddon has come—not with a bang, but a checkbook. The Vegan must die. There is no alternative. Help us stop him."

"What do you want of me?"

"Let Hasan destroy him."

"No."

"Why not? What is he to you?"

"Nothing, really. In fact, I dislike him very much. But what is he to *you?*"

"Our destroyer."

"Then tell me why, and how, and perhaps I'll give you a better answer."

"I can't."

"Why not?"

"Because I don't know."

"Then good night. That's all."

"Wait! I really do not know—but the word has come down from Taler, from the Radpol liaison there: He must die. His book is not a book, his self is not a self, but many. I do not know what this means but our agents have never lied before. You've lived on Taler, you've lived on Bakab and a dozen other worlds. You are Karaghiosis. You know that our agents do not lie, because you are Karaghiosis and you established the spy-circuit yourself. Now you hear their words and you do not heed them. I tell you that they say he must die. He represents the end of everything we've fought for. They say he is a surveyor who must not be permitted to survey. You know the code. Money against Earth. More Vegan exploitation. They could not specify beyond that point."

"I'm sorry. I've pledged myself to his defense. Give me a better reason and maybe I'll give you a better answer.—And Hasan tried to kill me."

"He was told only to stop you, to incapacitate you so that we could destroy the Vegan."

"Not good enough; not good enough, no. I admit nothing. Go your ways. I will forget."

"No, you must help us. What is the life of one Vegan to Karaghiosis?"

"I will not countenance his destruction without a just and specific cause. Thus far, you have shown me nothing."

"That's all I have."

"Then good night."

"No. You have two profiles. From the right side you are a demigod; from the left you are a demon. One of them will help us, must help us. I don't care which one it is."

"Do not try to harm the Vegan. We will protect him."

We sat there. She took one of my cigarettes and we sat there smoking.

". . . Hate you," she said after a time. "It should be easy, but I can't."

I said nothing.

"I've seen you many times, swaggering in your Dress Blacks, drinking rum like water, confident of something you never share, arrogant in your strength.—You'd fight your weight in anything that moves, wouldn't you?"

"Not red ants or bumblebees."

"Do you have some master plan of which we

know nothing? Tell us, and we will help you with it."

"It is your idea that I am Karaghiosis. I've explained why Hasan called me by that name. Phil knew Karaghiosis and you know Phil. Has he ever said anything about it?"

"You know he hasn't. He is your friend and he would not betray your confidence."

"Is there any other indication of identity than Hasan's random name-calling?"

"There is no recorded description of Karaghiosis. You were quite thorough."

"All right then. Go away and don't bother me."

"Don't. Please."

"Hasan tried to kill me."

"Yes; he must have thought it easier to kill you than to try keeping you out of the way. After all, he knows more about you than we do."

"Then why did he save me from the boadile today, along with Myshtigo?"

"I'd rather not say."

"Then forget it."

"No, I will tell you.—The *assagai* was the only thing handy. He is not yet proficient with it. He was not aiming to hit the boadile."

"Oh."

"But he was not aiming at you, either. The beast was writhing too much. He wanted to kill the Vegan, and he would simply have said that he had tried to save you both, by the only means at hand—and that there had been a terrible accident. Unfortunately, there was no terrible accident. He missed his target."

"Why did he not just let the boadile kill him?"

"Because you had already gotten your hands

upon the beast. He feared you might still save him. He fears your hands."

"That's nice to know. Will he continue trying, even if I refuse to cooperate?"

"I'm afraid so."

"That is very unfortunate, my dear, because I will not permit it."

"You will not stop him. Neither will we call him off. Even though you are Karaghiosis, and hurt, and my sorrow for you overflows the horizons, Hasan will not be stopped by you or by me. He *is* the Assassin. He has never failed."

"Neither have I."

"Yes you have. You have just failed the Radpol and the Earth, and everything that means anything."

"I keep my own counsel, woman. Go your ways."

"I can't."

"Why is that?"

"If you don't know, then Karaghiosis is indeed the fool, the buffoon, the figure in a shadow play."

"A man named Thomas Carlyle once wrote of heroes and hero-worship. He too was a fool. He believed there were such creatures. Heroism is only a matter of circumstances and expediency."

"Ideals occasionally enter into the picture."

"What is an ideal? A ghost of a ghost, that's all."

"Do not say these things to me, please."

"I must—they are true."

"You lie, Karaghiosis."

"I do not—or if I do, it is for the better, girl."

"I am old enough to be anyone's grandmother but yours, so do not call me 'girl.' Do you know that my hair is a wig?"

"Yes."

"Do you know that I once contracted a Vegan disease—and that that is why I must wear a wig?"

"No. I am very sorry. I did not know."

"When I was young, long ago, I worked at a Vegan resort. I was a pleasure girl. I have never fogotten the puffing of their horrid lungs against my body, nor the touch of their corpse-colored flesh. I hate them, Karaghiosis, in ways that only one such as you could understand—one who has hated all the great hates."

"I am sorry, Diane. I am so sorry that it hurts you still. But I am not yet ready to move. Do not push me."

"You *are* Karaghiosis?"

"Yes."

"Then I am satisfied—somewhat."

"But the Vegan *will* live."

"We shall see."

"Yes, we shall. Good night."

"Good night, Conrad."

And I rose, and I left her there, and I returned to my tent. Later that night she came to me. There was a rustling of the tent flap and the bedclothes, and she was there. And when I have forgotten everything else about her—the redness of her wig and the little upside-down "v" between her eyes, and the tightness of her jaws, and her clipped talk, and all her little mannerisms of gesture, and her body warm as the heart of a star, and her strange indictment of the man I once might have been, I will remember this—that she came to me when I needed her, that she was warm, soft, and that she came to me. . . .

After breakfast the following morning I was going

to seek Myshtigo, but he found me first. I was down by the river, talking with the men who would be taking charge of the felucca.

"Conrad," he said softly, "may I speak with you?"

I nodded and gestured toward a gully.

"Let's walk up this way. I've finished here."

We walked.

After a minute he said, "You know that on my world there are several systems of mental discipline, systems which occasionally produce extrasensory abilities. . . ."

"So I've heard," I said.

"Most Vegans, at sometime or other, are exposed to it. Some have an aptitude along these lines. Many do not. Just about all of us, though, possess a feeling for it, a recognition of its operations."

"Yes?"

"I am not telepathic myself, but I am aware that you possess this ability because you used it on me last night. I could feel it. It is quite uncommon among your people, so I had not anticipated this and I had taken no precautions to prevent it. Also, you hit me at the perfect moment. As a result, my mind was opened to you. I have to know how much you learned."

So there apparently had been something extrasensory connected with those sight-vision overlays. All they usually contained were what seemed the immediate perceptions of the subject, plus a peek at the thoughts and feelings that went into the words he made—and sometimes I got them wrong. Myshtigo's question indicated that he did not know how far mine went, and I had heard that some professional Veggy psyche-stirrers could even elbow their way into the unconscious. So I decided to bluff.

"I gather that you are not writing a simple travel book," I said.

He said nothing.

"Unfortunately, I am not the only one who is aware of this," I continued, "which places you in a bit of danger."

"Why?" he asked suddenly.

"Perhaps they misunderstand," I ventured.

He shook his head.

"Who are they?"

"Sorry."

"But I need to know."

"Sorry again. If you want out, I can get you back to the Port today."

"No, I can't do that. I must go on. What am I to do?"

"Tell me a little more about it, and I'll make suggestions."

"No, you know too much already. . . .

"Then that must be the real reason Donald Dos Santos is here," he said quickly. "He is a moderate. The activist wing of the Radpol must have learned something of this and, as you say—misunderstood. He must know of the danger. Perhaps I should go to him . . ."

"No," I said quickly, "I don't think you should. It really wouldn't change anything. What would you tell him, anyhow?"

A pause. Then, "I see what you mean," he said. "The thought has also occurred to me that he might not be as moderate as I have believed. . . . If that is the case, then—"

"Yeah," I said. "Want to go back?"

"I can't."

"Okay then, blue boy, you're going to have to trust *me.* You can start by telling me more about this survey—"

"No! I do not know how much you know and how much you do not know. It is obvious that you are trying to elicit more information, so I do not think you know very much. What I am doing is still confidential."

"I am trying to protect you," I said, "therefore I want as much information as I can get."

"Then protect my body and let me worry about my motives and my thoughts. My mind will be closed to you in the future, so you needn't waste your time trying to probe it."

I handed him an automatic.

"I suggest you carry a weapon for the duration of the tour—to protect your motives."

"Very well."

It vanished beneath his fluttering shirt.

Puff-puff-puff, went the Vegan.

Damn-damn-damn, went my thoughtstrings.

"Go get ready," I said. "We'll be leaving soon."

As I walked back toward the camp, via another route, I analyzed my own motives. A book, alone, could not make or break the Earth, the Radpol, Returnism. Even Phil's *Call of Earth* had not done that, not really. But this thing of Myshtigo's was to be more than just a book. A survey?—What could it be? A push in what direction? I did not know and I had to know. For Myshtigo could not be permitted to live if it would destroy us—and yet, I could not permit his destruction if the thing might be of any help at all. And it might.

Therefore, someone had to call time-out until we could be sure.

The leash had been tugged. I followed.

"Diane," said I, as we stood in the shade of her Skimmer, "you say that I mean something to you, as me, as Karaghiosis."

"That would seem to follow."

"Then hear me. I believe that you *may* be wrong about the Vegan. I am not sure, but if you are wrong it would be a very big mistake to kill him. For this reason, I cannot permit it. Hold off on anything you've planned until we reach Athens. Then request a clarification of that message from the Radpol."

She stared me in both eyes, then said, "All right."

"Then what of Hasan?"

"He waits."

"He makes his own choice as to time and place, does he not? He awaits only the opportunity to strike."

"Yes."

"Then he must be told to hold off until we know for sure."

"Very well."

"You will tell him?"

"He will be told."

"Good enough."

I turned away.

"And when the message comes back," she said, "if it should say the same thing as before—what then?"

"We'll see," I said, not turning.

I left her there beside her Skimmer and returned to my own.

When the message did come back, saying what I thought it would say, I knew that I would have more trouble on my hands. This was because I had already made my decision.

Far to the south and east of us, parts of Madagascar still deafened the geigs with radioactive pain-cries—a tribute to the skill of one of us.

Hasan, I felt certain, could still face any barrier without blinking those sun-drenched, death-accustomed, yellow eyes . . .

He might be hard to stop.

It. Down below.

Death, heat, mud-streaked tides, new shorelines. . . .

Vulcanism on Chios, Samos, Ikaria, Naxos. . . .

Halicarnassos bitten away. . . .

The western end of Kos visible again, but so what?

. . . Death, heat, mud-streaked tides.

New shorelines. . . .

I had brought my whole convoy out of its way in order to check the scene. Myshtigo took notes, also photos.

Lorel had said, "Continue on with the tour. Damage to property has not been too severe, because the Mediterranean was mostly full of junkstuff. Personal injuries were either fatal or are already being taken of.—So continue on."

I skimmed in low over what remained of Kos—the westward tail of the island. It was a wild, volcanic country, and there were fresh craters, fuming ones, amidst the new, bright sea-laces that crisscrossed over the land. The ancient capital of

Astypalaia had once stood there. Thucydides tells us it had been destroyed by a powerful earthquake. He should have seen this one. My norhtern city of Kos had then been inhabited from 366 B.C. Now all was gone but the wet and the hot. There were no survivors—and the plane tree of Hippocrates and the mosque of the Loggia and the castle of the Knights of Rhodes, and the fountains, and my cottage, and my wife—swept by what tides or caught in what sea-pits, I do not know—had gone the ways of dead Theocritus—he who had done his best to immortalize the place so many years before. Gone. Away. Far. . . . Immortal and dead to me. Further east, a few peaks of that high mountain range which had interrupted the northern coastal plain were still poking themselves up out of the waters. There was the mighty peak of Dhikaios, or Christ the Just, which had overlooked the villages of the northern slopes. Now it was a tiny islet, and no one had made it up to the top in time.

It must have been like this, that time so many years ago, when the sea near my homeland, bounded by the Chalcidic peninsula, had risen up and assaulted the land; in that time when the waters of the inland sea had forced them an outlet through the gorge of Tempe, the mighty convulsions of the thing scoring even the mountain walls of the home of the gods itself, Olympus; and those it spared were only Mr. and Mrs. Deukalion, kept afloat by the gods for purposes of making a myth and some people to tell it to.

"You lived there," said Myshtigo.

I nodded.

"You were born in the village of Makrynitsa, though, in the hills of Thessaly?"

"Yes."

"But you made your home there?"

"For a little while."

"'Home' is a universal concept," said he. "I appreciate it."

"Thanks."

I continued to stare downward, feeling sad, bad, mad, and then nothing.

Athens after absence returns to me with a sudden familiarity which always refreshes, often renews, sometimes incites. Phil once read me some lines by one of the last great Greek poets, George Seferis, maintaining that he had referred to my Greece when he said, ". . . A country that is no longer our own country, nor yours either"—because of the Vegans. When I pointed out that there were no Vegans available during Seferis' lifetime, Phil retorted that poetry exists independent of time and space and that it means whatever it means to the reader. While I have never believed that a literary license is also good for time-travel, I had other reasons for disagreeing, for not reading it as a general statement.

It *is* our country. The Goths, the Huns, the Bulgars, the Serbs, the Franks, the Turks, and lately the Vegans have never made it go way from us. People, I have outlived. Athens and I have changed together, somewhat. Mainland Greece, though, is mainland Greece, and it does not change for me. Try talking it away, whatever you are, and my klephtes will stalk the hills, like the chthonic avengers of old. You will pass, but the hills of Greece will remain, will be unchanged, with the smell of goat thigh-bones burning, with a mingling of blood and wine, a taste of sweetened almonds, a cold wind by night, and skies as bluebright as the eyes of a god by day. Touch them, if you dare.

That is why I am refreshed whenever I return, because now that I am a man with many years behind me, I feel this way about the entire Earth. That is why I fought, and why I killed and bombed, and why I tried every legal trick in the book, too, to stop the Vegans from buying up the Earth, plot by plot, from the absentia government, there on Taler. That is why I pushed my way, under another new name, into the big civil service machine that runs this planet—and why Arts, Monuments and Archives, in particular. There, I could fight to preserve what still remained, while I waited for the next development.

The Radpol vendetta had frightened the expatriates as well as the Vegans. They did not realize that the descendants of those who had lived through the Three Days would not willingly relinquish their best areas of coastline for Vegan resorts, nor yield up their sons and daughters to work in those resorts; nor would they guide the Vegans through the ruins of their cities, indicating points of interest for their amusement. That is why the Office is mainly a foreign service post for most of its staff.

We had sent out the call of return to those descendants of the Martian and Titanian colonies, and there had been no return. They had grown soft out there, soft from leeching on a culture which had had a headstart on ours. They lost their identity. They abandoned us.

Yet, they were the Earthgov, *de jure*, legally elected by the absent majority—and maybe *de facto* too, if it ever came to that. Probably so. I hoped it wouldn't come to that.

For over half a century there had been a stalemate. No new Veggy resorts, no new Radpol violence. No Return, either. Soon there would be a new development. It was in the air—if Myshtigo was really surveying.

So I came back to Athens on a bleak day, during a cold, drizzling rainfall, an Athens rocked and rearranged by the recent upheavals of Earth, and there was a question in my head and bruises on my body, but I was refreshed. The National Museum still stood there between Tossisa and Vasileos Irakliou, the Acropolis was even more ruined than I remembered, and the Garden Altar Inn—formerly the old Royal Palace—there at the northwest corner of the National Gardens, across from Syndagma Square, had been shaken but was standing and open for business, despite.

We entered, and checked in.

As Commissioner of Arts, Monuments and Archives, I received special considerations. I got The Suite: Number 19.

It wasn't exactly the way I'd left it. It was clean and neat.

The little metal plate on the door said:

This suite was the headquarters of Konstantin Karaghiosis during the founding of the Radpol and much of the Returnist Rebellion.

Inside, there was a plaque on the bedstead which read:

Konstantin Karaghiosis slept in this bed.

In the long, narrow front room I spotted one on the far wall. It said:

The stain on this wall was caused by a bottle of beverage, hurled across the room by Konstantin Karaghiosis, in celebration of the bombing of Madagascar.

Believe that, if you want to.

Konstantin Karaghiosis sat in this chair, insisted anoher.

I was really afraid to go into the bathroom.

Later that night, as I walked the wet and rubble-strewn pavements of my almost deserted city, my old memories and my current thoughts were like the coming together of two rivers. I'd left the others snoring inside, descended the wide stairway from the Altar, paused to read one of the inscriptions from Perikles' funeral oration—"The entire Earth is the tomb of great men"—there on the side of the Memorial to the Unknown Soldier, and I studied for a moment those great-thewed limbs of that archaic warrior, laid out with all his weapons on his funeral bed, all marble and bas-relief, yet somehow almost warm, because night becomes Athens—and then I walked on by, passing up Leoforos Amalias.

It had been a fine dinner: ouzo, giuvetsi, Kokkineli, yaourti, Metaxa, lots of dark coffee, and Phil arguing with George about evolution.

"Do you not see a convergence of life and myth, here, during the last days of life on this planet?"

"What do you mean?" asked George, polishing off a mess of narantzi and adjusting his glasses for peering.

"I mean that as humanity rose out of darkness it brought with it legends and myths and memories of fabulous creatures. Now we are descending again into that same darkness. The Life Force grows weak and unstable, and there is a reversion to those primal forms which for so long existed only as dim racial memories—"

"Nonsense, Phil. Life Force? In what century do you make your home? You speak as though all of life were one single, sentient entity."

"It is."

"Demonstrate, please."

"You have the skeletons of three satyrs in your museum, and photographs of live ones. They live in the hills of this country.

"Centaurs, too, have been seen here—and there are vampire flowers, and horses with vestigial wings. There are sea serpents in every sea. Imported spiderbats plow our skies. There are even sworn statements by persons who have seen the black Beast of Thessaly, an eater of men, bones and all—and all sorts of other legends are coming alive."

George sighed.

"What you have said so far proves nothing other than that in all of infinity there is a possibility for any sort of life form to put in an appearance, given the proper precipitating factors and a continuous congenial environment. The things you have mentioned which are native to Earth are mutations, creatures originating near various Hot Spots about the world. There is one such place up in the hills of Thessaly. If the Black Beast were to crash through that door at this moment, with a satyr mounted on its back, it would not alter my opinion, nor prove yours."

I'd looked at the door at that moment, hoping not for the Black Beast, but for some inconspicuous-looking old man who might sidle by, stumble, and pass on, or for a waiter bringing Diane an unordered drink with a note folded inside the napkin.

But none of these things happened. As I passed up Leoforos Amalias, by Hadrian's Gate, and past the Olympieion, I still did not know what the word was to be. Diane had contacted the Radpol, but there had been no response as yet. Within another thirty-six hours we would be skimming from Athens to Lamia, then onward by foot through areas of strange new trees with long, pale, red-veined leaves, hanging vines, and things that brachiate up above, and all the budding places of the *strige-fleur* down among their roots; and then on, across sun-washed plains, up twisty goat trails, through high, rocky places, and down deep ravines, past ruined monasteries. It was a crazy notion, but Myshtigo, again, had wanted it that way. Just because I'd been born there, he thought he'd be safe. I'd tried to tell him of the wild beasts, of the cannibal Kouretes—the tribesmen who wandered there. But he wanted to be like Pausanius and see it all on foot. Okay then, I decided, if the Radpol didn't get him, then the fauna would.

But, just to be safe, I had gone to the nearest Earthgov Post Office, obtained a dueling permit, and paid my death-tax. I might as well be on the up-and-up about these things, I decided, me being a Commissioner and all.

If Hasan needed killing, I'd kill him legally.

I heard the sound of a bouzouki coming from a small cafe on the other side of the street. Partly because I wanted to, and partly because I had a feeling that I was being followed, I crossed over and entered the place. I moved to a small table where I could keep my back to the wall and my eyes on the door, ordered Turkish coffee, ordered a package of cigarettes, listened to the songs of death, exile, disaster, and the eternal faithlessness of women and men.

It was even smaller inside than it had seemed from the street—low ceiling, dirt floor, real dark. The singer was a squat woman, wearing a yellow dress and much mascara. There was a rattling of glasses; a steady fall of dust descended through the dim air; the sawdust was damp underfoot. My table was set at the near end of the bar. There were maybe a dozen other people spotted about the place: three sleepy-eyed girls sat drinking at the bar, and a man wearing a dirty fez, and a man resting his head on an outstretched arm, and snoring; four men were laughing at a table diagonally across from me; a few others, solitary, were drinking coffee, listening, watching nothing in particular, waiting, or maybe not waiting, for something or someone to happen.

Nothing did, though. So after my third cup of coffee, I paid the fat, moustached owner his tab, and left the place.

Outside, the temperature seemed to have dropped several degrees. The street was deserted, and quite dark. I turned right into Leoforos Dionysiou Areopagitou and moved on until I reached the battered fence that runs along the southern slope of the Acropolis.

I heard a footfall, way back behind me, at the corner. I stood there for half a minute, but there was only silence and very black night. Shrugging, I entered the gate and moved to the tenemos of Dionysius Eleutherios. Nothing remains of the temple itself but the foundation. I passed on, heading toward the Theater.

Phil, then, had suggested that history moved in great cycles, like big clock hands passing the same numbers day after day.

"Historical biology proves you wrong," said George.

"I didn't mean *literally,*" replied Phil.

"Then we ought to agree on the language we are speaking before we talk any further."

Myshtigo had laughed.

Ellen touched Dos Santos' arm and asked him about the poor horses the picadores rode. He had shrugged, poured her more Kokkineli, drank his own.

"It is a part of the thing," he'd said.

And no message, no message. . . .

I walked on through the mess time makes of greatness. A frightened bird leapt up on my right, uttered a frightened cry, was gone. I kept walking, wandered into the old Theater at last, moved downward through it. . . .

Diane was not so amused as I had thought she would be by the stupid plaques that decorated my suite.

"But they belong here. Of course. They do."

"Ha!"

"At one time it would have been the heads of animals you had slain. Or the shields of your vanquished enemies. We're civilized now. This is the new way."

"Ha! again." I changed the subject. "Any word on the Vegan?"

"No."

"You want *his* head."

"I'm not civilized.—Tell me, was Phil always such a fool, back in the old days?"

"No, he wasn't. Isn't now, either. His was the curse of a half-talent. Now he is considered the last of the Romantic poets, and he's gone to seed. He pushes his mysticism into nonsense because, like Wordsworth, he has outlived his day. He lives now in distortions of a pretty good past.

"Like Byron, he once swam the Hellespont, but now, rather like Yeats, the only thing he really enjoys is the company of young ladies whom he can bore with his philosophy, or occasionally charm with a well-told reminiscence. He is old. His writing occasionally shows flashes of its former power, but it was not just his writing that was his whole style."

"How so?"

"Well, I remember one cloudy day when he stood in the Theater of Dionysius and read a hymn to Pan which he had written. There was an audience of two or three hundred—and only the gods know why they showed up—but he began to read.

"His Greek wasn't very good yet, but his voice was quite impressive, his whole manner rather charismatic. After a time, it began to rain, lightly, but no one left. Near the end there was a peal of thunder, sounding awfully like laughter, and a sudden shudder ran through the crowd. I'm not saying that it was like that in the days of Thespis, but a lot of those people were looking over their shoulders as they left.

"I was very impressed also. Then, several days later, I read the poem—and it was nothing, it was doggerel, it was trite. It was the way he did it that was important. He lost that part of his power along with his youth, and what remained of what might be called art was not strong enough to make him great, to keep alive his personal legend. He resents this, and he consoles himself with obscure philosophy, but in answer to your question—no, he was not always such a fool."

"Perhaps even some of his philosophy is correct."

"What do you mean?"

"The Big Cycles. The age of strange beasts *is* come upon us again. Also, the age of heroes, demigods."

"I've only met the strange beasts."

"'Karaghiosis slept in this bed,' it says here. Looks comfortable."

"It is.—See?"

"Yes. Do I get to keep the plaque?"

"If you want. . . ."

I moved to the proskenion. The relief sculpture-work started at the steps, telling tales from the life of Dionysius. Every tour guide and every member of a tour must, under a regulation promulgated by me, ". . . carry no fewer than three magnesium flares on his person, while traveling." I pulled the pin from one and cast it to the ground. The dazzle would not be visible below, because of the angle of the hillside and the blocking masonry.

I did not stare into the bright flame, but above, at the silver-limned figures. There was Hermes, presenting the infant god to Zeus, while the Corybantes tripped the Pyrrhic fantastic on either side of the throne; then there was Ikaros, whom Dionysius had taught to cultivate the vine—he was preparing to sacrifice a goat, while his daughter was offering cakes to the god (who stood aside, discussing her with a satyr); and there was drunken Silenus, attempting to hold up the sky like Atlas, only not doing so well; and there were all the other gods of the cities, paying a call to this Theater—and

I spotted Hestia, Theseus, and Eirene with a horn of plenty. . . .

"You burn an offering to the gods," came a statement from nearby.

I did not turn. It had come from behind my right shoulder, but I did not turn because I knew the voice.

"Perhaps I do," I said.

"It has been a long time since you walked this land, this Greece."

"That is true."

"Is it because there has never been an immortal Penelope—patient as the mountains, trusting in the return of her kallikanzaros—weaving, patient as the hills?"

"Are you the village story-teller these days?"

He chuckled.

"I tend the many-legged sheep in the high places, where the fingers of Aurora come first to smear the sky with roses."

"Yes, you're the story teller. Why are you not up in the high places now, corrupting youth with your song?"

"Because of dreams."

"Aye."

I turned and looked into the ancient face—its wrinkles, in the light of the dying flare, as black as fishers' nets lost at the bottom of the sea, the beard as white as the snow that comes drifting down from the mountains, the eyes matching the blue of the headcloth corded about his temples. He did not lean upon his staff any more than a warrior leans on his spear. I knew that he was over a century old, and that he had never taken the S-S series.

"A short time ago did I dream that I stood in the

midst of a black temple," he told me, "and Lord Hades came and stood by my side, and he gripped my wrist and bade me to go with him. But I said 'Nay' and I awakened. This did trouble me."

"What did you eat that night? Berries from the Hot Place?"

"Do not laugh, please.—Then, of a later night, did I dream that I stood in a land of sand and darkness. The strength of the old champions was upon me, and I did battle with Antaeus, son of the Earth, destroying him. Then did Lord Hades come to me again, and taking me by the arm did say, 'Come with me now.' But again did I deny him, and I awakened. The Earth was a-tremble."

"That's all?"

"No. Then, more recent still, and not at night, but as I sat beneath a tree watching my flock, did I dream a dream while awake. Pheobus-like did I battle the monster Python, and was almost destroyed thereby. This time Lord Hades did not come, but when I turned about there stood Hermes, his lackey, smiling and pointing his caducaeus like a rifle in my direction. I shook my head and he lowered it. Then he raised it once more in a gesture, and I looked where he had indicated.

"There before me lay Athens—this place, this Theater, you—and here sat the old women. The one who measures out the thread of life was pouting, for she had wrapped yours about the horizon and no ends were in sight. But the one who weaves had divided it into two very thin threads. One strand ran back across the seas and vanished again from sight. The other led up into the hills. At the first hill stood the Dead Man, who held your thread in his white, white hands. Beyond him, at the next hill, it lay across a burning rock. On the hill beyond the rock stood the Black Beast, and he shook and worried your thread with his teeth.

"And all along the length of the strand stalked a great foreign warrior, and yellow were his eyes and naked the blade in his hands, and he did raise this blade several times in menace.

"So I came down to Athens—to meet you, here, at this place—to tell you to go back across the seas —to warn you not to come up into the hills where death awaits you. For I knew, when Hermes raised his wand, that the dreams were not mine, but they were meant for you, oh my father, and that I must find you here and warn you. Go away now, while still you can. Go back. Please."

I gripped his shoulder.

"Jason, my son, I do not turn back. I take full responsibility for my own actions, right or wrong—including my own death, if need be—and I *must* go into the hills this time, up near the Hot Place. Thank you for your warning. Our family has always had this thing with dreams, and often it is misleading. I, too, have dreams—dreams in which I see through the eyes of other persons—sometimes clearly, sometimes not so clearly. Thank you for your warning. I am sorry that I must not heed it."

"Then I will return to my flock."

"Come back with me to the inn. We will fly you as far as Lamia tomorrow."

"No. I do not sleep in great buildings, nor do I fly."

"Then it's probably time you started, but I'll humor you. We can camp here tonight. I'm Commissioner of this monument."

"I had heard you were important in the Big Government again. Will there be more killing?"

"I hope not."

We found a level place and reclined upon his cloak.

"How do you interpret the dreams?" I asked him.

"Your gifts do come to us with every season, but when was the last time you yourself visited?"

"It was about nineteen years ago," I said.

"Then you do not know of the Dead Man?"

"No."

"He is bigger than most men—taller, fatter—with flesh the color of a fishbelly, and teeth like an animal's. They began telling of him about fifteen years ago. He comes out only at night. He drinks blood. He laughs a child's laugh as he goes about the countryside looking for blood—people's, animals', it does not matter. He smiles in through bedroom windows late at night. He burns churches. He curdles milk. He causes miscarriages from fright. By day, it is said that he sleeps in a coffin, guarded by the Kourete tribesmen."

"Sounds as bad as a kallikanzaros."

"He really exists, father. Some time ago, something had been killing my sheep. Whatever it was had partly eaten them and drunk much of their blood. So I dug me a hiding place and covered it over with branches. That night I watched. After many hours he came, and I was too afraid to put a stone in my sling—for he is as I have described him: big, bigger than you even, and gross, and colored like a fresh-dug corpse. He broke the sheep's neck with his hands and drank the blood from its throat. I wept to see it, but I was afraid to do anything. The next day I moved my flock and was not troubled again. I use the story to frighten my great-grandchildren—your great-great-grandchildren—whenever they misbehave.—And he is waiting, up in the hills."

"Mm, yes. . . . If you say you saw it, it must be true. And strange things do come out of the Hot Places. *We* know that."

". . . Where Prometheus spilled too much of the fire of creation!"

"No, where some bastard lobbed a cobalt bomb and the bright-eyed boys and girls cried 'Eloi' to the fallout.—And what of the Black Beast?"

"He too, is real, I am certain. I have never seen him, though. The size of an elephant, and very fast—and eater of flesh, they say. He haunts the plains. Perhaps some day he and the Dead Man will meet and they will destroy one another."

"It doesn't usually work out that way, but it's a nice thought.—That's all you know about him?"

"Yes, I know of no one who has caught more than a glimpse."

"Well, I shall try for less than that."

". . . And then I must tell you of Bortan."

"Bortan? That name is familiar."

"Your dog. I used to ride on his back when I was a child and beat with my legs upon his great armored sides. Then he would growl and seize my foot, but gently."

"*My* Bortan has been dead for so long that he would not even chew upon his own bones, were he to dig them up in a modern incarnation."

"I had thought so, too. But two days after you departed from your last visit, he came crashing into the hut. He apparently had followed your trail across half of Greece."

"You're sure it was Bortan?"

"Was there ever another dog the size of a small horse, with armor plates on his sides, and jaws like a trap for bears?"

"No, I don't think so. That's probably why the species died out. Dogs do need armor plating if they're going to hang around with people, and they didn't develop it fast enough. If he is still alive, he's probably the last dog on Earth. He and I were puppies together, you know, so long ago that it hurts to think about it. That day he vanished while we were hunting I thought he'd had an accident. I searched for him, then decided he was dead. He was incredibly old at the time."

"Perhaps he was injured, and wandering that way—for years. But he was himself and he followed your track, that last time. When he saw that you were gone, he howled and took off after you again. We have never seen him since then. Sometimes, though, late at night, I hear his hunting-cry in the hills. . . ."

"The damn fool mutt ought to know it's not right to care for anything that much."

"Dogs were strange."

"Yes, dogs were."

And then the night wind, cool through arches of the years, came hounding after me. It touched my eyes.

Tired, they closed.

Greece is lousy with legend, fraught with menace. Most areas of mainland near the Hot Place are historically dangerous. This is because, while the Office theoretically runs the Earth, it actually only tends to the islands. Office personnel on much of the mainland are rather like twentieth-century Revenue Officers were in certain hill areas. They're fair game in all seasons. The islands sustained less damage than the rest of the world during the Three Days, and consequently they were the logical outposts for world district offices when the Talerites decided we could use some administration. Historically, the mainlanders have always been opposed to this. In the regions about the Hot Places, though, the natives are not always completely human. This compounds the historical antipathy with abnormal behavior patterns. This is why Greece is fraught.

We could have sailed up the coast to Volos. We could have skimmed to Volos—or almost anywhere else, for that matter. Myshtigo wanted to hike from Lamia, though, to hike and enjoy the refreshment of legend and alien scenery. This is why we left the Skimmers at Lamia. This is why we hiked to Volos.

This is why we encountered legend.

I bade Jason goodbye in Athens. He was sailing up the coast. Wise.

Phil had insisted on enduring the hike, rather than skimming ahead and meeting us up further long the line. Good thing, too, maybe, in a way, sort of. . . .

The road to Volos wanders through the thick and the sparse in the way of vegetation. It passes huge boulders, occasional clusters of shacks, fields of poppies; it crosses small streams, winds about hills, sometimes crosses over hills, widens and narrows without apparent cause.

It was still early morning. The sky was somehow a blue mirror, because the sunlight seemed to be coming from everywhere. In places of shade some moisture still clung to the grasses and the lower leaves of the trees.

It was in an interesting glade along the road to Volos that I met a half-namesake.

The place had once been a shrine of some sort, back in the Real Old Days. I came to it quite often in my youth because I liked the quality of—I guess you'd call it "peace"—that it contained. Sometimes I'd meet the half-people or the no-people there, or dream good dreams, or find old pottery or the heads of statues, or things like that, which I could sell down in Lamia or in Athens.

There is no trail that leads to it. You just have to know where it is. I wouldn't have taken them there, except for the fact that Phil was along and I knew that he liked anything which smacks of an adytum, a sequestered significance, a sliding-panel view onto dim things past, etcetera.

About half a mile off the road, through a small forest, self-content in its disarray of green and shade and its haphazard heaps of stone, you suddenly go downhill, find the way blocked by a thick thicket, push on through, then discover a blank wall of rock. If you crouch, keep close to that wall, and bear to the right, you then come upon a glade where it is often well to pause before proceeding further.

There is a short, sharp drop, and down below is an eggshaped clearing, about fifty meters long, twenty across, and the small end of the egg butting into a bitten-out place in the rock; there is a shallow cave at the extreme end, usually empty. A few half-sunken, almost square stones stand about in a seemingly random way. Wild grapevines grow around the perimeter of the place, and in the center is an enormous and ancient tree whose branches act as an umbrella over almost the entire area, keeping it dusky throughout the day. Because of this, it is hard to see into the place even from the glade.

But we could see a satyr in the middle, picking his nose.

I saw George's hand go to the mercy-gun he carried. I caught his shoulder, his eyes, shook my head. He shrugged, and nodded, dropping his hand.

I withdrew from my belt the shepherd's pipe I had asked Jason to give me. I motioned to the others to crouch and remain where they were. I moved a few steps further ahead and raised the syrinx to my lips.

My first notes were quite tentative. It had been too long since I'd played the pipes.

His ears pricked forward and he looked all about him. He made rapid moves in three different directions—like a startled squirrel, uncertain as to which tree to make for.

Then he stood there quivering as I caught up an old tune and nailed it to the air.

I kept playing, remembering, remembering the pipes, the tunes, and the bitter, the sweet, and the drunken things I've really always known. It all came back to me as I stood there playing for the little guy in the shaggy leggings: the fingering and the control of the air, the little runs, the thorns of sound, the things only the pipes can really say. I can't play in the cities, but suddenly I was me again, and I saw faces in the leaves and I heard the sound of hooves.

I moved forward.

Like in a dream, I noticed I was standing with my back against the tree, and they were all about me. They shifted from hoof to hoof, never staying still, and I played for them as I had so often before, years ago, not knowing whether they were really the same ones who'd heard me then—or caring, actually. They cavorted about me. They laughed through white, white teeth and their eyes danced, and they circled, jabbing at the air with their horns, kicking their goat legs high off the ground, bending far forward, springing into the air, stamping the earth.

I stopped, and lowered the pipes.

It was not an human intelligence that regarded me from those wild, dark eyes, as they all froze into statues, just standing there, staring at me.

I raised the pipes once more, slowly. This time I played the last song I'd ever made. I remembered it so well. It was a dirge-like thing I had played on the night I'd decided Karaghiosis should die.

I had seen the fallacy of Return. They would not come back, would never come back. The Earth would die. I had gone down into the Gardens and played this one last tune I'd learned from the wind and maybe even the stars. The next day, Karaghiosis' big blazeboat had broken up in the bay at Piraeus.

They seated themselves on the grass. Occasionally, one would dab at his eye with an elaborate gesture. They were all about me, listening.

How long I played, I do not know. When I had finished, I lowered the pipes and sat there. After a time, one of them reached out and touched the pipes and drew his hand back quickly. He looked up at me.

"Go," I said, but they did not seem to understand.

So I raised the syrinx and played the last few bars over again.

The Earth is dying, dying. Soon it will be dead. . . . Go home, the party's over. It's late, it's late, so late. . . .

The biggest one shook his head.

Go away, go away, go away now. Appreciate the silence. After life's most ridiculous gambit, appreciate the silence. What did the gods hope to gain, to gain? Nothing. 'Twas all but a game. Go away, go away, go away now. It's late, it's late, so late. . . .

They still sat there, so I stood up and clapped my hands, yelled "Go!" and walked away quickly.

I gathered my companions and headed back for the road.

It is about sixty-five kilometers from Lamia to Volos, including the detour around the Hot Spot. We covered maybe a fifth of that distance on the first day. That evening, we pitched our camp in a clearing off to the side of the road, and Diane came up beside me and said, "Well?"

"'Well' what?"

"I just called Athens. Blank. The Radpol is silent. I want your decision now."

"You are very determined. Why can't we wait some more?"

"We've waited too long as it is. Supposing he decides to end the tour ahead of schedule?—This countryside is perfect. So many accidents could come so easily here. . . . You know what the Radpol will say—the same as before—and it will signify the same as before: Kill."

"My answer is also the same as before: No."

She blinked rapidly, lowered her head.

"Why don't you give him his walking papers right now and save me some trouble?"

"I won't do that."

"I didn't think you would."

She looked up again. Her eyes were moist, but her face and voice were unchanged.

"If it should turn out that you were right and we were wrong," she said, "I am sorry."

"Me too," I said. "Very, very."

That night I dozed within knifing distance of Myshtigo, but nothing happened or tried to. The following morning was uneventful, as was most of the afternoon.

"I can't do that."

"Dos Santos does as you tell him."

"The problem is *not* an administrative one!—Damn it! I wish I'd never met you!"

"I'm sorry."

"The Earth is at stake and you're on the wrong side."

"I think you are."

"What are you going to do about it?"

"I can't convince you, so I'll just have to stop you."

"You couldn't turn in the Secretary of the Radpol and his consort without evidence. We're too ticklish politically."

"I know that."

"So you couldn't hurt Don, and I don't believe you'd hurt me."

"You're right."

"That leaves Hasan."

"Right again."

"And Hasan is—Hasan. What will you do?"

"Please reconsider."

"No."

"Then do this much," she said. "Forget it. The whole thing. Wash your hands of the affair. Take Lorel up on his offer and get us a new guide. You can skim out of here in the morning."

"No."

"Are you really serious, then—about protecting Myshtigo?"

"Yes."

"I don't want you hurt, or worse."

"I'm not particularly fond of the idea myself. So you can save us both a lot of trouble by calling it off."

"Myshtigo," I said, as soon as we paused for purposes of photographing a hillside, "why don't you go home? Go back to Taler? Go anywhere? Walk away from it? Write some other book? The further we get into civilization, the less is my power to protect you."

"You gave me an automatic, remember?" he said.

He made a shooting motion with his right hand.

"All right—just thought I'd give it another try."

"That's a goat standing on the lower limb of that tree, isn't it?"

"Yeah; they like to eat those little green shoots that come up off the branches."

"I want a picture of that too. Olive tree, isn't it?"

"Yes."

"Good. I wanted to know what to call the picture. 'Goat eating green shoots in olive tree,'" he dictated; "that will be the caption."

"Great. Shoot while you have the chance."

If only he weren't so uncommunicative, so alien,

so unconcerned about his welfare! I hated him. I couldn't understand him. He wouldn't speak, unless it was to request information or to answer a question. Whenever he did answer questions, he was terse, elusive, insulting, or all three at once. He was smug, conceited, blue, and overbearing. It really made me wonder about the Shtigogens' tradition of philosophy, philanthrophy and enlightened journalism. I just didn't like him.

But I spoke to Hasan that evening, after having kept an eye (the blue one) on him all day.

He was sitting beside the fire, looking like a sketch by Delacroix. Ellen and Dos Santos sat nearby, drinking coffee, so I dusted off my Arabic and approached.

"Greetings."

"Greetings."

"You did not try to kill me today."

"No."

"Tomorrow, perhaps?"

He shrugged.

"Hasan—look at me."

He did.

"You were hired to kill the blue one."

He shrugged again.

"You needn't deny it, or admit it. I already know. I cannot allow you to do this thing. Give back the money Dos Santos has paid you and go your way. I can get you a Skimmer by morning. It will take you anywhere in the world you wish to go."

"But I am happy here, Karagee."

"You will quickly cease being happy if any harm comes to the blue one."

"I am a bodyguard, Karagee."

"No, Hasan. You are the son of a dyspeptic camel."

"What is 'dyspeptic,' Karagee?"

"I do not know the Arabic word, and you would not know the Greek one. Wait, I'll find another insult.—You are a coward and a carrion-eater and a skulker up alleyways, because you are half jackal and half ape."

"This may be true, Karagee, because my father told me that I was born to be flayed alive and torn into quarters."

"Why was that?"

"I was disrespectful to the Devil."

"Oh?"

"Yes.—Were those devils that you played music for yesterday? They had the horns, the hooves . . ."

"No, they were not devils. They were the Hot-born children of unfortunate parents who left them to die in the wilderness. They lived, though, because the wilderness is their real home."

"Ah! And I had hoped that they were devils. I still think they were, because one smiled at me as I prayed to them for forgiveness."

"Forgiveness? For what?"

A faraway look came into his eyes.

"My father was a very good and kind and religious man," he said. "He worshipped Malak Tawus, whom the benighted Shi'ites" (he spat here) "calls Iblis—or Shaitan, or Satan—and he always paid his respects to Hallaj and the others of the Sandjaq. He was well-known for his piety, his many kindnesses.

"I loved him, but as a boy I had an imp within me. I was an atheist. I did not believe in the Devil.

And I was an evil child, for I took me a dead chicken and mounted it on a stick and called it the Peacock Angel, and I mocked it with stones and pulled its feathers. One of the other boys grew frightened and told my father of this. My father flogged me then, in the streets, and he told me I was born to be flayed alive and torn into quarters for my blasphemies. He made me go to Mount Sandjar and pray for forgiveness, and I went there—but the imp was still within me, despite the flogging, and I did not really believe as I prayed.

"Now that I am older the imp has fled, but my father too, is gone—these many years—and I cannot tell him: I am sorry that I mocked the Peacock Angel. As I grow older I feel the need for religion. I hope that the Devil, in his great wisdom and mercy—understands this and forgives me."

"Hasan, it is difficult to insult you properly," I said. "But I warn you—the blue one must not be harmed."

"I am but a humble bodyguard."

"Ha! Yours is the cunning and the venom of the serpent. You are deceitful and treacherous. Vicious, too."

"No, Karagee. Thank you, but it is not true. I take pride in always meeting my commitments. That is all. This is the law I live by. Also, you cannot insult me so that I will challenge you to a duel, permitting you to choose bare hands or daggers or sabers. No. I take no offense."

"Then beware," I told him. "Your first move toward the Vegan will be your last."

"If it is so written, Karagee . . ."

"And call me Conrad!"

I stalked away, thinking bad thoughts.

* * *

The following day, all of us still being alive, we broke camp and pushed on, making about eight kilometers before the next interruption occurred.

"That sounded like a child crying," said Phil.

"You're right."

"Where is it coming from?"

"Off to the left, down there."

We moved through some shrubbery, came upon a dry stream bed, and followed it around a bend.

The baby lay among the rocks, partly wrapped in a dirty blanket. Its face and hands were already burnt red from the sun, so it must have been there much of the day before. The bite-marks of many insects were upon its tiny, wet face.

I knelt, adjusting the blanket to cover it better.

Ellen cried a little as the blanket fell open in front and she saw the baby.

There was a natural fistula in the child's chest, and something was moving inside.

Red Wig screamed, turned away, began to weep.

"What is it?" asked Myshtigo.

"One of the abandoned," I said. "One of the marked ones."

"How awful!" said Red Wig.

"Its appearance? Or the fact that it was abandoned?" I asked.

"Both!"

"Give it to me," said Ellen.

"Don't touch it," said George, stooping. "Call for a Skimmer," he ordered. "We have to get it to a hospital right away. I don't have the equipment to operate on it here.—Ellen, help me."

She was at his side then, and they went through his medkit together.

"You write what I do and pin the note onto a clean blanket—so the doctors in Athens will know."

Dos Santos was phoning Lamia by then, to pick up on one of our Skimmers.

And then Ellen was filling hypos for George and swabbing the cuts and painting the burns with unguents and writing it all down. They shot the baby full of vitamins, antibiotics, general adaptives, and half a dozen other things. I lost count after awhile. They covered its chest with gauze, sprayed it with something, wrapped it in a clean blanket, and pinned the note to it.

"What a dreadful thing!" said Dos Santos. "Abandoning a deformed child, leaving it to die in such a manner!"

"It's done here all the time," I told him, "especially about the Hot Places. In Greece there has always been a tradition of infanticide. I myself was exposed on a hilltop on the day I was born. Spent the night there, too."

He was lighting a cigarette, but he stopped and stared at me.

"You? Why?"

I laughed, glanced down at my foot.

"Complicated story. I wear a special shoe because this leg is shorter than the other. Also, I understand I was a very hairy baby—and then, my eyes don't match. I suppose I might have gotten by if that had been all, but then I went and got born on Christmas and that sort of clinched things."

"What is wrong with being born on Christmas?"

"The gods, according to local beliefs, deem it a bit presumptuous. For this reason, children born at that time are not of human blood. They are of the brood of destroyers, the creators of havoc, the panickers of man. They are called the kallikanzaroi. Ideally, they look something like those guys with horns and hooves and all, but they don't have to. They could look like me, my parents decided—if they *were* my parents. So they left me on a hilltop, to be returned."

"What happened then?"

"There was an old Orthodox priest in the village. He heard of it and went to them. He told them that it was a mortal sin to do such a thing, and they had better get the baby back, quick, and have it ready for baptism the following day."

"Ah! And that is how you were saved, and baptised?"

"Well, sort of." I took one of his cigarettes. "They came back with *me,* all right, but they insisted I wasn't the same baby they'd left there. They'd left a dubious mutant and collected an even more doubtful changeling, they said. Uglier too, they claimed, and they got another Christmas child in return. Their baby had been a satyr, they said, and they figured that perhaps some Hot creature had had a sort of human child and had abandoned it in the same way we do them—making a swap, actually. Nobody had seen me before then, so their story couldn't be checked. The priest would have none of this, though, and he told them they were stuck with me. But they were very kind, once they were reconciled to the fact. I grew fairly large fairly young, and I was strong for my age. They liked that."

"And you were baptised . . . ?"

"Well, sort of half-baptised."

"Half-baptised?"

"This priest had a stroke at my christening. Died

a little while later. He was the only one around, so I don't know that I got the whole thing done proper."

"One drop would be sufficient."

"I suppose so. I don't really know what happened."

"Maybe you had better have it done again. Just to be safe."

"No, if Heaven didn't want me then, I'm not going to ask a second time."

We set up a beacon in a nearby clearing and waited for the Skimmer.

We made another dozen or so kilometers that day, which was pretty good, considering the delay. The baby had been picked up and dispatched directly to Athens. When the Skimmer had set down, I'd asked in a large voice whether anyone else wanted a ride back. There'd been no takers, though.

And it was that evening that it happened.

We reclined about a fire. Oh, it was a jolly fire, flapping its bright wing against the night, warming us, smelling woody, pushing a smoke-stack into the air. . . . Nice.

Hasan sat there cleaning his aluminum-barreled shotgun. It had a plastic stock and it was real light and handy.

As he worked on it, it tilted forward, moved slowly about, pointed itself right at Myshtigo.

He'd done it quite neatly, I must admit that. It was during a period of over half an hour, and he'd advanced the barrel with almost imperceptible movements.

I snarled, though, when its position registered in

my cerebrum, and I was at his side in three steps.

I struck it from his hands.

It clattered on some small stone about eight feet away. My hand was stinging from the slap I'd given it.

Hasan was on his feet, his teeth shuttling around inside his beard, clicking together like flint and steel. I could almost see the sparks.

"Say it!" I cried. "Go ahead, say something! Anything! You know damn well what you were just doing!"

His hands twitched.

"Go ahead!" I said. "Hit me! Just touch me, even. Then what I do to you will be self-defense, provoked assault. Even George won't be able to put you back together again."

"I was only cleaning my shotgun. You've damaged it."

"*You* do not point weapons by accident. You were going to kill Myshtigo."

"You are mistaken."

"Hit me. Or are you a coward?"

"I have no quarrel with you."

"You *are* a coward."

"No, I am not."

After a few seconds he smiled.

"Are you afraid to challenge *me?*" he asked.

And there it was. The only way.

The move had to be mine. I had hoped it wouldn't have to be that way. I had hoped that I could anger him or shame him or provoke him into striking me or challenging me.

I knew then that I couldn't.

Which was bad, very bad.

I was sure I could take him with anything I cared

to name. But if he had it his way, things could be different. Everybody knows that there are some people with an aptitude for music. They can hear a piece once and sit down and play it on the piano or thelinstra. They can pick up a new instrument, and inside a few hours they can sound as if they've been playing it for years. They're good, very good at such things, because they have that talent—the ability to coordinate a special insight with a series of new actions.

Hasan was that way with weapons. Maybe some other people could be the same, but they don't go around doing it—not for decades and decades, anyway, with everything from boomerangs to blowguns. The dueling code would provide Hasan with the choice of means, and he was the most highly skilled killer I'd ever known.

But I had to stop him, and I could see that this was the only way it could be done, short of murder. I had to take him on his terms.

"Amen," I said. "I challenge you to a duel."

His smile remained, grew.

"Agreed—before these witnesses. Name your second."

"Phil Graver. Name yours."

"Mister Dos Santos."

"Very good. I happen to have a dueling permit and the registration forms in my bag, and I've already paid the death-tax for one person. So there needn't be much of a delay. When, where, and how do you want it?"

"We passed a good clearing about a kilometer back up the road."

"Yes; I recall it."

"We shall meet there at dawn tomorrow."

"Check," I said. "And as to weapons . . . ?"

He fetched his knapcase, opened it. It bristled with interesting sharp things, glistened with ovoid incendiaries, writhed with coils of metal and leather.

He withdrew two items and closed the pack.

My heart sank.

"The sling of David," he announced.

I inspected them.

"At what distance?"

"Fifty meters," he said.

"You've made a good choice," I told him, not having used one in over a century myself. "I'd like to borrow one tonight, to practice with. If you don't want to lend it to me, I can make my own."

"You may take either, and practice all night with it."

"Thanks." I selected one and hung it from my belt. Then I picked up one of our three electric lanterns. "If anybody needs me, I'll be up the road at the clearing," I said. "Don't forget to post guards tonight. This is a rough area."

"Do you want me to come along?" asked Phil.

"No. Thanks anyway. I'll go alone. See you."

"Then good night."

I hiked back along the way, coming at last to the clearing. I set up the lantern at one end of the place, so that it reflected upon a stand of small trees, and I moved to the other end.

I collected some stones and slung one at a tree. I missed.

I slung a dozen more, hitting with four of them.

I kept at it. After about an hour, I was hitting with a little more regularity. Still, at fifty meters I probably couldn't match Hasan.

The night wore on, and I kept slinging. After a time, I reached what seemed to be my learning plateau for accuracy. Maybe six out of seven of my shots were coming through.

But I had one thing in my favor, I realized, as I twirled the sling and sent another stone smashing into a tree. I delivered my shots with an awful lot of force. Whenever I was on target there was much power behind the strike. I had already shattered several of the smaller trees, and I was sure Hasan couldn't do that with twice as many hits. If I could reach him, fine; but all the power in the world was worthless if I couldn't connect with it.

And I was sure he could reach me. I wondered how much of a beating I could take and still operate.

It would depend, of course, on where he hit me.

I dropped the sling and yanked the automatic gun from my belt when I heard a branch snap, far off to my right. Hasan came into the clearing.

"What do you want?" I asked him.

"I came to see how your practice was going," he said, regarding the broken trees.

I shrugged, reholstered my automatic and picked up the sling.

"Comes the sunrise and you will learn."

We walked across the clearing and I retrieved the lantern. Hasan studied a small tree which was now, in part, toothpicks. He did not say anything.

We walked back to the camp. Everyone but Dos Santos had turned in. Don was our guard. He paced about the warning perimeter, carrying an automatic rifle. He waved to him and entered the camp.

Hasan always pitched a Gauzy—a one-molecule-layer tent, opaque, feather-light, and very tough. He never slept in it, though. He just used it to stash his junk.

I seated myself on a log before the fire and Hasan ducked inside his Gauzy. He emerged a moment later with his pipe and a block of hardened, resinous-looking stuff, which he proceeded to scale and grind. He mixed it with a bit of burley and then filled the pipe.

After he got it going with a stick from the fire, he sat smoking it beside me.

"I do not want to kill you, Karagee," he said.

"I share this feeling. I do not wish to be killed."

"But we must fight tomorrow."

"Yes."

"You could withdraw your challenge."

"You could leave by Skimmer."

"I will not."

"Nor will I withdraw my challenge."

"It is sad," he said, after a time. "Sad, that two such as we must fight over the blue one. He is not worth your life, nor mine."

"True," I said, "but it involves more than just his life. The future of this planet is somehow tied up with whatever he is doing."

"I do not know of these things, Karagee. I fight for money. I have no other trade."

"Yes, I know."

The fire burnt low. I fed it more sticks.

"Do you remember the time we bombed the Coast of Gold, in France?" he asked.

"I remember."

"Beside the blue ones, we killed many people."

"Yes."

"The future of the planet was not changed by this, Karagee. For here we are, many years away from the thing, and nothing is different."

"I know that."

"And do you remember the days when we crouched in a hole on a hillside, overlooking the bay at Piraeus? Sometimes you would feed me the belts and I would strafe the blazeboats, and when I grew tired you would operate the gun. We had much ammunition. The Office Guard did not land that day, nor the next. They did not occupy Athens, and they did not break the Radpol. And we talked as we sat there, those two days and that night, waiting for the fireball to come—and you told me of the Powers in the Sky."

"I forget. . . ."

"I do not. You told me that there are men, like us, who live up in the air by the stars. Also, there are the blue ones. Some of the men, you said, seek the blue ones' favor, and they would sell the Earth to them to be made into a museum. Others, you said, did not want to do this thing, but they wanted it to remain as it is now—their property, run by the Office. The blue ones were divided among themselves on this matter, because there was a question as to whether it was legal and ethical to do this thing. There was a compromise, and the blue ones were sold some clean areas, which they used as resorts, and from which they toured the rest of the Earth. But you wanted the Earth to belong only to people. You said that if we gave the blue ones an inch, then they would want it all. You wanted the men by the stars to come back and rebuild the cities, bury the Hot Places, kill the beasts which prey upon men.

"As we sat there, waiting for the fireball, you said that we were at war, not because of anything we could see or hear or feel or taste, but because of the Powers in the Sky, who had never seen us, and whom we would never see. The Powers in the Sky had done this thing, and because of it men had to die here on Earth. You said that by the death of men and blue ones, the Powers might return to Earth. They never did, though. There was only the death.

"And it was the Powers in the Sky which saved us in the end, because they had to be consulted before the fireball could be burnt over Athens. They reminded the Office of an old law, made after the time of the Three Days, saying that the fireball would never again burn in the skies of Earth. You had thought that they would burn it anyhow, but they did not. It was because of this that we stopped them at Piraeus. I burnt Madagaskee for you, Karagee, but the Powers never came down to Earth. And when People get much money they go away from here—and they never come back from the sky. Nothing we did in those days has caused a change."

"Because of what we did, things remained as they were, rather than getting worse," I told him.

"What will happen if this blue one dies?"

"I do not know. Things may worsen then. If he is viewing the areas we pass through as possible real estate tracts, to be purchased by Vegans, then it is the old thing all over again."

"And the Radpol will fight again, will bomb them?"

"I think so."

"Then let us kill him now, before he goes further, sees more."

"It may not be that simple—and they would only send another. There would also be repercussions—perhaps mass arrests of Radpol members. The Radpol is no longer living on the edge of life as it was in those days. The people are unready. They need time to prepare. This blue one, at least, I hold in my hand. I can watch him, learn of his plans. Then, if it becomes necessary, I can destroy him myself."

He drew on his pipe. I sniffed. It was something like sandalwood that I smelled.

"What are you smoking?"

"It comes from near my home. I visited there recently. It is one of the new plants which has never grown there before. Try it."

I took several mouthfuls into my lungs. At first there was nothing. I continued to draw on it, and after a minute there was a gradual feeling of coolness and tranquility which spread down through my limbs. It tasted bitter, but it relaxed. I handed it back. The feeling continued, grew stronger. It was very pleasant. I had not felt that sedate, that relaxed, for many weeks. The fire, the shadows, and the ground about us suddenly became more real, and the night air and the distant moon and the sound of Dos Santos' footsteps came somehow more clearly than life, really. The struggle seemed ridiculous. We would lose it in the end. It was written that humanity was to be the cats and the dogs and trained chimpanzees of the real people, the Vegans—and in a way it was not such a bad idea. Perhaps we needed someone wiser to watch over us, to run our lives. We had made a shambles of our own world during the Three Days, and the Vegans had never had a nuclear war. They operated a smoothly efficient interstellar government, encompassing dozens of planets. Whatever they did was esthetically pleasing. Their own lives were well-regulated, happy things. Why not let them have the Earth? They'd probably do a better job with it than we'd ever done. And why not be their coolies, too? It wouldn't be a bad life. Give them the old ball of mud, full of radioactive sores and populated by cripples.

Why not?

I accepted the pipe once more, inhaled more peace. It was so pleasant not to think of these things at all, though. Not to think of anything you couldn't really do anything about. Just to sit there and breathe in the night and be one with the fire and the wind was enough. The universe was singing its hymn of oneness. Why open the bag of chaos there in the cathedral?

But I had lost my Cassandra, my dark witch of Kos, to the mindless powers which move the Earth and the waters. Nothing could kill my feelings of loss. It seemed further away, somehow insulated behind glass, but it was still there. Not all the pipes of the East could assuage this thing. I did not want to know peace. I wanted hate. I wanted to strike out at all the masks in the universe—earth, water, sky, Taler, Earthgov, and Office—so that behind one of them I might find that power which had taken her, and make it too, know something of pain. I did not want to know peace. I did not want to be at one with anything which had harmed that which was mine, by blood and by love. For just five minutes even, I wanted to be Karaghiosis again, looking at it all through crosshairs and squeezing a trigger.

Oh, Zeus, of the hot red lightnings, I prayed, give it to me that I may break the Powers in the Sky!

I returned to the pipe again.

"Thank you, Hasan, but I'm not ready for the Bo Tree."

I stood then and moved off toward the place where I had cast my pack.

"I am sorry that I must kill you in the morning," he called after me.

Sipping beer in a mountain lodge on the planet Divbah, with a Vegan seller of information named Krim (who is now dead), I once looked out through a wide window and up at the highest mountain in the known universe. It is called Kasla, and it has never been climbed. The reason I mention it is because on the morning of the duel I felt a sudden remorse that I had never attempted to scale it. It is one of those crazy things you think about and promise yourself that someday you're going to try, and then you wake up one morning and realize that it is probably exactly too late: you'll never do it.

There were no-expressions on every face that morning.

The world outside us was bright and clear and clean and filled with the singing of birds.

I had forgotten the use of the radio until after the duel, and Phil carried some of its essential entrails in his jacket pocket, just to be sure.

Lorel would not know. The Radpol would not know. Nobody would know, until after.

The preliminaries completed, the distance was measured off.

We took our places at the opposite ends of the clearing. The rising sun was to my left.

"Are you ready, gentlemen?" called out Dos Santos.

"Yes," and "I am," were the replies.

"I make a final attempt to dissuade you from this course of action. Do either of you wish to reconsider?"

"No," and "No."

"Each of you has ten stones in similar size and weight. The first shot is, of course, given to he who was challenged: Hasan."

We both nodded.

"Proceed, then."

He stepped back and there was nothing but fifty meters of air separating us. We both stood sideways, so as to present the smallest target possible. Hasan fitted his first stone to the sling.

I watched him wind it rapidly through the air behind him, and suddenly his arm came forward.

There was a crashing sound in back of me.

Nothing else happened.

He'd missed.

I put a stone to my own sling then and whipped it back and around. The air sighed as I cut it all apart.

Then I hurled the missile forward with all the strength of my right arm.

It grazed his left shoulder, barely touching it. It was mostly garment that it plowed.

The stone ricocheted from tree to tree behind him, before it finally vanished.

All was still then. The birds had given up on their morning concert.

"Gentlemen," called Dos Santos, "you have each had one chance to settle your differences. It may be said that you have faced one another with honor, given vent to your wrath, and are now satisfied. Do you wish to stop the duel?"

"No," said I.

Hasan rubbed his shoulder, shook his head.

He put the second stone to his sling, worked it rapidly through a powerful windup, then released it at me.

Right between the hip and the ribcage, that's where it caught me.

I fell to the ground and it all turned black.

A second later the lights came on again, but I was doubled up and something with a thousand teeth had me by the side and wouldn't let go.

They were running toward me, all of them, but Phil waved them back.

Hasan held his position.

Dos Santos approached.

"Is that it?" asked Phil softly. "Can you get up?"

"Yeah. I need a minute to breathe and to put the fire out, but I'll get up."

"What is the situation?" asked Dos Santos.

Phil told him.

I put my hand to my side and stood again, slowly.

A couple inches higher or lower and something boney might have broken. As it was, it just hurt like blazes.

I rubbed it, moved my right arm through a few circles to test the play of muscles on that side. Okay.

Then I picked up the sling and put a stone to it.

This time it would connect. I had a feeling.

It went around and around and it came out fast.

Hasan toppled, clutching at his left thigh.

Dos Santos went to him. They spoke.

Hasan's robe had muffled the blow, had partly deflected it. The leg was not broken. He would continue as soon as he could stand.

He spent five minutes massaging it, then he got to his feet again. During that time my pain had subsided to a dull throbbing.

Hasan selected his third stone.

He fitted it slowly, carefully . . .

He took my measure. Then he began to lash at the air with the sling. . . .

All the while I had the feeling—and it kept growing—that I should be leaning a little further to the right. So I did.

He twirled it, threw it.

It grazed my fungus and tore at my left ear.

Suddenly my cheek was wet.

Ellen screamed, briefly.

A little further to the right, though, and I wouldn't have been hearing her.

It was my turn again.

Smooth, gray, the stone had the feel of death about it. . . .

I will be it, this one seemed to say.

It was one of those little premonitory tuggings at my sleeve, of the sort for which I have a great deal of respect.

I wiped the blood from my cheek. I fitted the stone.

There was death riding in my right arm as I raised it. Hasan felt it too, because he flinched. I could see this from across the field.

"You will all remain exactly where you are, and drop your weapons," said the voice.

It said it in Greek, so no one but Phil and Hasan

and I understood it, for sure. Maybe Dos Santos or Red Wig did. I'm still not certain.

But all of us understood the automatic rifle the man carried, and the swords and clubs and knives of the three dozen or so men and half-men standing behind him.

They were Kouretes.

Kouretes are bad.

They always get their pound of flesh.

Usually roasted.

Sometimes fried, though.

Or boiled, or raw. . . .

The speaker seemed to be the only one carrying a firearm.

. . . And I had a handful of death circling high above my shoulder. I decided to make him a gift of it.

His head exploded as I delivered it.

"Kill them!" I said, and we began to do so.

George and Diane were the first to open fire. Then Phil found a handgun. Dos Santos ran for his pack. Ellen got there fast, too.

Hasan had not needed my order to begin killing. The only weapons he and I were carrying were the slings. The Kouretes were closer than our fifty meters, though, and theirs was a mob formation. He dropped two of them with well-placed stones before they began their rush. I got one more, also.

Then they were halfway across the field, leaping over their dead and their fallen, screaming as they came on toward us.

Like I said, they were not all of them human: there was a tall, thin one with three-foot wings covered with sores, and there were a couple microcephalics with enough hair so that they looked headless, and there was one guy who should probably have been twins, and then several steatopygiacs, and three huge, hulking brutes who kept coming despite bullet-holes in their chests and abdomens; one of these latter had hands which must have been twenty inches long and a foot across, and another appeared to be afflicted with something like elephantiasis. Of the rest, some were reasonably normal in form, but they all looked mean and mangy and either wore rags or no rags at all and were unshaven and smelled bad, too.

I hurled one more stone and didn't get a chance to see where it hit, because they were upon me then.

I began lashing out—feet, fists, elbows; I wasn't too polite about it. The gunfire slowed down, stopped. You have to stop to reload sometime, and there'd been some jamming, too. The pain in my side was a very bad thing. Still, I managed to drop three of them before something big and blunt caught me on the side of the head and I fell as a dead man falls.

Coming to in a stiflingly hot place. . . .

Coming to in a stiflingly hot place that smells like a stable. . . .

Coming to in a dark, stiflingly hot place that smells like a stable. . . .

. . . This is not real conducive to peace of mind, a settled stomach, or the resumption of sensory activities on a sure and normal keel.

It stank in there and it was damn hot, and I didn't really want to inspect the filthy floor too closely—it was just that I was in a very good position to do so.

I moaned, numbered all my bones, and sat up.

The ceiling was low and it slanted down even lower before it met with the back wall. The one window to the outside was small and barred.

We were in the back part of a wooden shack. There was another barred window in the opposite wall. It didn't look out on anything, though; it looked in. There was a larger room beyond it, and George and Dos Santos were talking through it with someone who stood on that other side. Hasan lay unconscious or dead about four feet away from me; there was dried blood on his head. Phil and Myshtigo and the girls were talking softly in the far corner.

I rubbed my temple while all this was registering within. My left side ached steadily, and numerous other portions of my anatomy had decided to join in the game.

"He's awake," said Myshtigo suddenly.

"Hi, everybody. I'm back again," I agreed.

They came toward me and I assumed a standing position. This was sheer bravado, but I managed to carry it.

"We are prisoners," said Myshtigo.

"Oh, yeah? Really? I'd never have guessed."

"Things like this do not happen on Taler," he observed, "or on any of the worlds in the Vegan Combine."

"Too bad you didn't stay there," I said. "Don't forget the number of times I asked you to go back."

"This thing would not have occurred if it had not been for your duel."

I slapped him then. I couldn't bring myself to slug him. He was just too pathetic. I hit him with the back of my hand and knocked him over into the wall.

"Are you trying to tell me you don't know why I stood there like a target this morning?"

"Because of your quarrel with my bodyguard," he stated, rubbing his cheek.

"—Over whether or not he was going to kill you."

"Me? Kill . . . ?"

"Forget it," I said. "It doesn't really matter anyhow. Not now. You're still on Taler, and you may as well stay there for your last few hours. It would have been nice if you could have come to Earth and visited with us for awhile. But things didn't work out that way."

"We are going to die here, aren't we?" he asked.

"That is the custom of the country."

I turned away and studied the man who was studying me from the other side of the bars. Hasan was leaning against the far wall then, holding his head. I hadn't noticed his getting up.

"Good afternoon," said the man behind the bars, and he said it in English.

"*Is* it afternoon?" I asked.

"Quite," he replied.

"Why aren't we dead?" I asked him.

"Because I wanted you alive," he stated. "Oh, not you personally—Conrad Nomikos, Commissioner of Arts, Monuments and Archives—and all your distinguished friends, including the poet laureate. I wanted any prisoners whom they came upon brought back alive. Your identities are, shall we say, condiments."

"To whom do I have the pleasure of speaking?" I asked.

"This is Doctor Moreby," said George.

"He is their witch doctor," said Dos Santos.

"I prefer 'Shaman' or 'Medicine Chief,' " corrected Moreby, smiling.

I moved closer to the grillwork and saw that he was rather thin, well-tanned, clean-shaven, and had all his hair woven into one enormous black braid which was coiled like a cobra about his head. He had close-set eyes, dark ones, a high forehead, and lots of extra jaw reaching down past his Adam's apple. He wore woven sandals, a clean green sari; and a necklace of human fingerbones. In his ears were big snake-shaped circlets of silver.

"Your English is rather precise," said I, "and 'Moreby' is not a Greek name."

"Oh goodness!" He gestured gracefully, in mock surprise. "I'm not a local! How could you ever mistake me for a local?"

"Sorry," I said; "I can see now that you're too well-dressed."

He giggled.

"Oh, *this* old rag . . . I just threw it on. —No, I'm from Taler. I read some wonderfully rousing literature on the subject of Returnism, and I decided to come back and help rebuild the Earth."

"Oh? What happened then?"

"The Office was not hiring at the time, and I experienced some difficulty in finding employment locally. So I decided to engage in research work. This place is full of opportunities for that."

"What sort of research?"

"I hold two graduate degrees in cultural anthropology, from New Harvard. I decided to study a Hot tribe in depth—and after some blandishments I got this one to accept me. I started out to educate them, too. Soon, though, they were deferring to me, all over the place. Wonderful for the ego.

After a time, my studies, my social work, came to be of less and less importance. Well, I daresay you've read *Heart of Darkness*—you know what I mean. The local practices are so—well, basic. I found it much more stimulating to participate than to observe. I took it upon myself to redesign some of their grosser practices along more esthetic lines. So I did really educate them, after all. They do things with ever so much style since I've come here."

"*Things?* Such as?"

"Well, for one thing, they were simple cannibals before. For another, they were rather unsophisticated in their use of their captives prior to slaying them. Things like that are quite important. If they're done properly they give you class, if you know what I mean. Here I was with a wealth of customs, superstitions, taboos—from many cultures, many eras—right here, at my fingertips." He gestured again. "Man—even half-man, Hot man—is a ritual-loving creature, and I knew ever so many rituals and things like that. So I put all of this to good use and now I occupy a position of great honor and high esteem."

"What are you trying to tell me about *us?*" I asked.

"Things were getting rather dull around here," he said, "and the natives were waxing restless. So I decided it was time for another ceremony. I spoke with Procrustes, the War Chief, and suggested he find us some prisoners. I believe it is on page 577 of the abridged edition of *The Golden Bough* that it states, 'The Tolalaki, notorious head-hunters of Central Celebes, drink the blood and eat the brains of their victims that they may become brave. The Italones of the Philippine Islands drink the blood of their slain enemies, and eat part of the back of their heads and their entrails raw to acquire their courage.' Well, we have the tongue of a poet, the blood of two very formidable warriors, the brains of a very distinguished scientist, the bilious liver of a fiery politician, and the interesting-colored flesh of a Vegan—all in this one room here. Quite a haul, I should say."

"You make yourself exceedingly clear," I observed. "What of the women?"

"Oh, for them we'll work out a protracted fertility rite ending in a protracted sacrifice."

"I see."

". . . That is to say, if we do not permit all of you to continue on your way, unmolested."

"Oh?"

"Yes. Procrustes likes to give people a chance to measure themselves against a standard, to be tested, and possibly to redeem themselves. He is most Christian in this respect."

"And true to his name, I suppose?"

Hasan came over and stood beside me, stared out through the grillwork at Moreby.

"Oh, good, good," said Moreby. "Really, I'd like to keep you around awhile, you know? You have a sense of humor. Most of the Kouretes lack this adjunct to what are otherwise exemplary personalities. I could learn to like you . . ."

"Don't bother. Tell me about the way of redemption, though."

"Yes. We are the wardens of the Dead Man. He is my most interesting creation. I am certain that one of you two shall realize this during your brief acquaintanceship with him." He glanced from me to Hasan to me to Hasan.

"I know of him" I said. "Tell me what must be done."

"You are called upon to bring forth a champion to do battle with him, this night, when he rises again from the dead."

"What is he?"

"A vampire."

"Crap. What is he really?"

"He is a genuine vampire. You'll see."

"Okay, have it your way. He's a vampire, and one of us will fight him. How?"

"Catch-as-catch-can, bare-handed—and he isn't very difficult to catch. He'll just stand there and wait for you. He'll be very thirsty, and hungry too, poor fellow."

"And if he is beaten, do your prisoners go free?"

"That is the rule, as I originally outlined it some sixteen or seventeen years ago. Of course, this contingency has never arisen. . . ."

"I see. You're trying to tell me he's tough."

"Oh, he's unbeatable. That's the fun of it. It wouldn't make for a good ceremony if it could end any other way. I tell the whole story of the battle before it takes place, and then my people witness it. It reaffirms their faith in destiny and my own close association with its workings."

Hasan glanced at me.

"What does he mean, Karagee?"

"It's a fixed fight," I told him.

"On the contrary," said Moreby, "it is not. It doesn't have to be. There was once an old saying on this planet, in connection with an ancient sport: Never bet against the damn Yankees, or you'll lose money. The Dead Man is unbeatable because he was born with a considerable amount of native ability, upon which I have elaborated, considerably. He has dined upon many champions, so of course his strength is equal to all of theirs. Everyone who's read Frazer knows that."

He yawned, covering his mouth with a feathered wand.

"I must go to the barbecue area now, to supervise the decking of the hall with boughs of holly. Decide upon your champion this afternoon, and I'll see you all this evening. Good day."

"Trip and break your neck."

He smiled and left the shack.

I called a meeting.

"Okay," I said, "they've got a weird Hot One called the Dead Man, who is supposed to be very tough. I am going to fight him tonight. If I can beat him we are supposed to go free, but I wouldn't take Moreby's word for anything. Therefore, we must plan an escape, else we will be served up on a chafing dish.

"Phil, do you remember the road to Volos?" I asked.

"I think so. It's been a long time. . . . But where are we now, exactly?"

"If it is of any help," answered Myshtigo, from beside the window, "I see a glowing. It is not any color for which there is a word in your language, but it is off in that direction." He pointed. "It is a color which I normally see in the vicinity of radioactive materials if the atmosphere is dense enough about them. It is spread over quite a large area."

I moved to the window and stared in that direction.

"That could be the Hot Spot, then," I said. "If

that is the case, then they've actually brought us further along toward the coast, which is good. Was anyone conscious when we were brought here?"

No one answered.

"All right. Then we'll operate under the assumption that that *is* the Hot Spot, and that we are very close to it. The road to Volos should be back that way, then." I pointed in the opposite direction. "Since the sun is on this side of the shack and it's afternoon, head in the other direction after you hit the road—away from the sunset. It might not be more than twenty-five kilometers."

"They will track us," said Dos Santos.

"There are horses," said Hasan.

"What?"

"Up the street, in a paddock. There were three near that rail earlier. They are back behind the edge of the building now. There may be more. They were not strong-looking horses, though."

"Can all of you ride?" I asked.

"I have never ridden a horse," said Myshtigo, "but the *thrid* is something similar. I have ridden *thrid.*"

Everyone else had ridden horses.

"Tonight then," I said. "Ride double if you must. If there are more than enough horses, then turn the others loose, drive them away. As they watch me fight the Dead Man you will make a break for the paddock. Seize what weapons you can and try to fight your way to the horses. —Phil, get them up to Makrynitsa and mention the name of Korones anywhere. They will take you in and protect you."

"I am sorry," said Dos Santos, "but your plan is not a good one."

"If you've got a better one, let's hear it," I told him.

"First of all," he said, "we cannot really rely on Mister Graber. While you were still unconscious he was in great pain and very weak. George believes that he suffered a heart attack during or shortly after our fight with the Kouretes. If anything happens to him we are lost. We will need you to guide us out of here, if we do succeed in breaking free. We *cannot* count on Mister Graber.

"Second," he said, "you are not the only man capable of fighting an exotic menace. Hasan will undertake the defeat of the Dead Man."

"I can't ask him to do that," I said. "Even if he wins, he will probably be separated from us at the time, and they'll doubtless get to him pretty fast. It would most likely mean his life. You hired him to kill for you, not to die."

"I will fight him, Karagee," he said.

"You don't have to."

"But I wish to."

"How are you feeling now, Phil?" I asked.

"Better, much better. I think it was just an upset stomach. Don't worry about it."

"Do you feel good enough to make it to Makrynitsa, on horseback?"

"No trick at all. It will be easier than walking. I was practically born on horseback. You remember."

" 'Remember'?" asked Dos Santos. "What do you mean by that, Mister Graber? How could Conrad remem—"

"—Remember his famous *Ballads on Horseback,*" said Red Wig. "What are you leading up to, Conrad?"

"I'm in charge here, thank you," said I. "I'm giving the orders and I've decided I'll do the vampire-fighting."

"In a situation like this I think we ought to be a little more democratic about these life and death decisions," she replied. "You were born in this country. No matter how good Phil's memory is, you'll do a better job of getting us from here to there in a hurry. You're not ordering Hasan to die, or abandoning him. He's volunteering."

"I will kill the Dead Man," said Hasan, "and I will follow after you. I know the ways of hiding myself from men. I will follow your trail."

"It's my job," I told him.

"Then, since we cannot agree, leave the decision to the fates," said Hasan. "Toss a coin."

"Very well. Did they take our money as well as our weapons?"

"I have some change," said Ellen.

"Toss a piece into the air."

She did.

"Heads," said I, as it fell toward the floor.

"Tails," she replied.

"Don't touch it!"

It was tails, all right. And there was a head on the other side, too.

"Okay, Hasan, you lucky fellow, you," I said. "You just won a do-it-yourself Hero Kit, complete with a monster. Good luck."

He shrugged.

"It was written."

He sat down then, his back against the wall, extracted a tiny knife from the sole of his left sandal, and began to pare his fingernails. He'd always been a pretty well-groomed killer. I guess cleanliness is next to diablerie, or something like that.

As the sun sank slowly in the west, Moreby came to us again, bringing with him a contingent of Kourete swordsmen.

"The time has come," he stated. "Have you decided upon your champion?"

"Hasan will fight him," I said.

"Very good. Then come along. Please do not try anything foolish. I should hate to deliver damaged goods at a festival."

Walking within a circle of blades, we left the shack and moved up the street to the village, passing by the paddock. Eight horses, heads low, stood within. Even in the diminishing light I could see that they were not very good horses. Their flanks were all covered with sores, and they were quite thin. Everyone glanced at them as we went by.

The village consisted of about thirty shacks, such as the one in which we had been confined. It was a dirt road that we walked on, and it was full of ruts and rubbish. The whole place smelled of sweat and urine and rotten fruit and smoke.

We went about eighty meters and turned left. It was the end of the street, and we moved along a downhill path into a big, cleared compound. A fat, bald-headed woman with enormous breasts and a face that was a lava field of carcinoma was tending a low and dreadfully suggestive fire at the bottom of a huge barbecue pit. She smiled as we passed by and smacked her lips moistly.

Great, sharpened stakes lay on the ground about her. . . .

Up further ahead was a level area of hardpacked bare earth. A huge, vine-infested, tropic-type tree which had adapted itself to our climate stood at the one end of the field, and all about the field's peripheries were rows of eight-foot torches, already waving great lengths of fire like pennants. At the other end was the most elaborate shack of them all. It was about five meters high and ten across the front. It was painted bright red and covered all over with Pennsylvania hex signs. The entire middle section of the front wall was a high, sliding door. Two armed Kouretes stood guard before that door.

The sun was a tiny piece of orange-rind in the west. Moreby marched us the length of the field toward the tree.

Eighty to a hundred spectators were seated on the ground on the other side of the torches, on each side of the field.

Moreby gestured, indicating the red shack.

"How do you like my home?" he asked.

"Lovely," said I.

"I have a roommate, but he sleeps during the day. You're about to meet him."

We reached the base of the big tree; Moreby left us there, surrounded by his guards. He moved to the center of the field and began addressing the Kouretes in Greek.

We had agreed that we would wait until the fight was near its end, whichever way, and the tribesmen all excited and concentrating on the finale, before we made our break. We'd pushed the women into the center of our group, and I managed to get on the left side of a right-handed swordsman, whom I intended to kill quickly. Too bad that we were at the far end of the field. To get to the horses we'd have to fight our way back through the barbecue area.

". . . and then, on that night," Moreby was

saying, "did the Dead Man rise up, smiting down this mighty warrior, Hasan, breaking his bones and casting him about this place of feasting. Finally, did he kill this great enemy and drink the blood from his throat and eat of his liver, raw and still smoking in the night air. These things did he do on that night. Mighty is his power."

"Mighty, oh mighty!" cried the crowd, and someone began beating upon a drum.

"Now will we call him to life again. . . ."

The crowd cheered.

"To life again!"

"To life again."

"To life again!"

"Hail!"

"Hail!"

"Sharp white teeth. . . ."

"Sharp white teeth!"

"White, white skin. . . ."

"White, white skin!"

"Hands which break. . . ."

"Hands which break!"

"Mouth which drinks. . . ."

"Mouth which drinks!"

"The blood of life!"

"The blood of life!"

"Great is our tribe!"

"Great is our tribe!"

"Great is the Dead Man!"

"Great is the Dead Man!"

"Great is the Dead Man!"

"GREAT IS THE DEAD MAN!"

They bellowed it, at the last. Throats human, half-human, and inhuman heaved the brief litany like a tidal wave across the field. Our guards, too, were screaming it. Myshtigo was blocking his sensitive ears and there was an expression of agony on his face. My head was ringing too. Dos Santos crossed himself and one of the guards shook his head at him and raised his blade meaningfully. Don shrugged and turned his head back toward the field.

Moreby walked up to the shack and struck three times upon the sliding door with his hand.

One of the guards pushed it open for him.

An immense black catafalque, surrounded by the skulls of men and animals, was set within. It supported an enormous casket made of dark wood and decorated with bright, twisting lines.

At Moreby's directions, the guards raised the lid.

For the next twenty minutes he gave hypodermic injections to something within the casket. He kept his movements slow and ritualistic. One of the guards put aside his blade and assisted him. The drummers kept up a steady, slow cadence. The crowd was very silent, very still.

Then Moreby turned.

"Now the Dead Man rises," he announced.

"Rises," responded the crowd.

"Now he comes forth to accept the sacrifice."

"Now he comes forth. . . ."

"Come forth, Dead Man," he called, turning back to the catafalque.

And he did.

At great length.

For he was big.

Huge, obese.

Great indeed was the Dead Man.

Maybe 350 pounds' worth.

He sat up in his casket and he looked all about

him. He rubbed his chest, his armpits, his neck, his groin. He climbed out of the big box and stood beside the catafalque, dwarfing Moreby.

He was wearing only a loincloth and large, goatskin sandals.

His skin was white, dead white, fishbelly white, moon white . . . dead white.

"An albino," said George, and his voice carried the length of the field, because it was the only sound in the night.

Moreby glanced in our direction and smiled. He took the Dead Man's stubby-fingered hand and led him out of the shack and onto the field. The Dead Man shied away from the torchlight. As he advanced, I studied the expression on his face.

"There is no intelligence in that face," said Red Wig.

"Can you see his eyes?" asked George, squinting. His glasses had been broken in the fray.

"Yes; they're pinkish."

"Does he have epicanthial folds?"

"Mm . . . Yeah."

"Uh-huh. He's a Mongoloid—an idiot, I'll wager—which is why it was so easy for Moreby to do what he's done with him. And look at his teeth! They look filed."

I did. He was grinning, because he'd seen the colorful top of Red Wig's head. Lots of nice, sharp teeth were exposed.

"His albinism is the reason behind the nocturnal habits Moreby has imposed. Look! He even flinches at the torchlight! He's ultrasensitive of any sort of antinics."

"What about his dietary habits?"

"Acquired, through imposition. Lots of primitive

people bled their cattle. The Kazaks did it until the twentieth century, and the Todas. You saw the sores on those horses as we passed by the paddock. Blood *is* nourishing, you know, if you can learn to keep it down—and I'm sure Moreby has regulated the idiot's diet since he was a child. So of course he's a vampire—he was brought up that way."

"The Dead Man is risen," said Moreby.

"The Dead Man is risen," agreed the crowd.

"Great is the Dead Man!"

"Great is the Dead Man!"

He dropped the dead-white hand then and walked toward us, leaving the only genuine vampire we knew of grinning in the middle of the field.

"Great is the Dead Man," he said, grinning himself as he approached us. "Rather magnificent, isn't he?"

"What have you done to that poor creature?" asked Red Wig.

"Very little," replied Moreby. "He was born pretty well-equipped."

"What were those injections you gave him?" inquired George.

"Oh, I shoot his pain centers full of Novocain before encounters such as this one. His lack of pain responses adds to the image of his invincibility. Also, I've given him a hormone shot. He's been putting on weight recently, and he's grown a bit sluggish. That compensates for it."

"You talk of him and treat him as though he's a mechanical toy," said Diane.

"He is. An invincible toy. An invaluable one, also.—You there, Hasan. Are you ready?" he asked.

"I am." Hasan answered, removing his cloak and

his burnoose and handing them to Ellen.

The big muscles in his shoulders bulged, his fingers flexed lightly, and he moved forward and out of the circle of blades. There was a welt on his left shoulder, several others on his back. The torchlight caught his beard and turned it to blood, and I could not help but remember that night back at the *hounfor* when he had enacted a strangling, and Mama Julie had said, "Your friend is possessed of Angelsou," and "Angelsou is a deathgod and he only visits with his own."

"Great is the Warrior, Hasan," announced Moreby, turning away from us.

"Great is the warrior, Hasan," replied the crowd.

"His strength is that of many."

"His strength is that of many," the crowd repeated.

"Greater still is the Dead Man."

"Greater still is the Dead Man."

"He breaks his bones and casts him about this place of feasting."

"He breaks his bones. . . ."

"He eats his liver."

"He eats his liver."

"He drinks the blood from his throat."

"He drinks the blood from his throat."

"Mighty is his power."

"Mighty is his power."

"Great is the Dead Man!"

"Great is the Dead Man!"

"Tonight," said Hasan quietly, "he becomes the Dead Man indeed."

"Dead Man!" cried Moreby, as Hasan moved forward and stood before him, "I give you this man Hasan in sacrifice!"

Then Moreby got out of the way and motioned the guards to move us to the far sideline.

The idiot grinned an even wider grin and reached out slowly toward Hasan.

"Bismallah," said Hasan, making as if to turn away from him, and bending downward and to the side.

He picked it off the ground and brought it up and around fast and hard, like a whiplash—a great heel-of-the-hand blow which landed on the left side of the Dead Man's jaw.

The white, white head moved maybe five inches.

And he kept on grinning. . . .

Then both of his short bulky arms came out and caught Hasan beneath the armpits. Hasan seized his shoulders, tracing fine red furrows up his sides as he went, and he drew red beads from the places where his fingers dug into snowcapped muscle.

The crowd screamed at the sight of the Dead Man's blood. Perhaps the smell of it excited the idiot himself. That, or the screaming.

Because he raised Hasan two feet off the ground and ran forward with him.

The big tree got in the way, and Hasan's head sagged as he struck.

Then the Dead Man crashed into him, stepped back slowly, shook himself, and began to hit him.

It was a real beating. He flailed at him with his almost grotesquely brief, thick arms.

Hasan got his hands up in front of his face and he kept his elbows in the pit of his stomach.

Still, the Dead Man kept striking him on his sides and head. His arms just kept rising and falling.

And he never stopped grinning.

Finally, Hasan's hands fell and he clutched them before his stomach.

. . . And there was blood coming from the corners of his mouth.

The invincible toy continued its game.

And then far, far off on the other side of the night, so far that only I could hear it, there came a voice that I recognized.

It was the great hunting-howl of my hellhound, Bortan.

Somewhere, he had come upon my trail, and he was coming now, running down the night, leaping like a goat, flowing like a horse or a river, all brindle-colored—and his eyes were glowing coals and his teeth were buzzsaws.

He never tired of runing, my Bortan.

Such as he are born without fear, given to the hunt, and sealed with death.

My hellhound was coming, and nothing could halt him in his course.

But he was far, so far off, on the other side of the night. . . .

The crowd was screaming. Hasan couldn't take much more of it. Nobody could.

From the corner of my eye (the brown one) I noticed a tiny gesture of Ellen's.

It was as though she had thrown something with her right hand. . . .

Two seconds later it happened.

I looked away quickly from that point of brilliance that occurred, sizzling, behind the idiot.

The Dead Man wailed, lost his grip.

Good old Reg 237.1 (promulgated by me):

"Every tour guide and every member of a tour must carry no fewer than three magnesium flares on his person, while traveling."

Ellen only had two left, that meant. Bless her.

The idiot had stopped hitting Hasan.

He tried to kick the flare away. He screamed. He tried to kick the flare away. He covered his eyes. He rolled on the ground.

Hasan watched, bleeding, panting. . . .

The flare burnt, the Dead Man screamed. . . .

Hasan finally moved.

He reached up and touched one of the thick vines which hung from the tree.

He tugged at it. It resisted. He pulled harder.

It came loose.

His movements were steadier as he twisted an end around each hand.

The flare sputtered, grew bright again. . . .

He dropped to his knees beside the Dead Man, and with a quick motion he looped the vine about his throat.

The flare sputtered again.

He snapped it tight.

The Dead Man fought to rise.

Hasan drew the thing tighter.

The idiot seized him about the waist.

The big muscles in the Assassin's shoulders grew into ridges. Perspiration mingled with the blood on his face.

The Dead Man stood, raising Hasan with him.

Hasan pulled harder.

The idiot, his face no longer white, but mottled, and with the veins standing out like cords in his forehead and neck, lifted him up off the ground.

As I'd lifted the golem did the Dead Man raise Hasan, the vine cutting ever more deeply into his neck as he strained with all his inhuman strength.

The crowd was wailing and chanting incoherently. The drumming, which had reached a frenzied throb, continued at its peak without letup. And then I heard the howl again, still very far away.

The flare began to die.

The Dead Man swayed.

. . . Then, as a great spasm racked him, he threw Hasan away from him.

The vine went slack about his throat as it tore free from Hasan's grip.

Hasan took *Ukemi* and rolled to his knees. He stayed that way.

The Dead Man moved toward him.

Then his pace faltered.

He began to shake all over. He made a gurgling noise and clutched at his throat. His face grew darker. He staggered to the tree and put forth a hand. He leaned there panting. Soon he was gasping noisily. His hand slipped along the trunk and he dropped to the ground. He picked himself up again, into a half-crouch.

Hasan arose, and recovered the piece of vine from where it had fallen.

He advanced upon the idiot.

This time his grip was unbreakable.

The Dead Man fell, and he did not rise again.

It was like turning off a radio which had been playing at full volume:

Click. . . .

Big silence then—it had all happened so fast. And tender was the night, yea verily, as I reached out through it and broke the neck of the swordsman at my side and seized his blade. I turned then to my left and split the skull of the next one with it.

Then, like *click* again, and full volume back on, but all static this time. The night was torn down through the middle.

Myshtigo dropped his man with a vicious rabbit-punch and kicked another in the shins. George managed a quick knee to the groin of the one nearest him.

Dos Santos, not so quick—or else just unlucky—took two bad cuts, chest and shoulder.

The crowd rose up from where it had been scattered on the ground, like a speedup film of beansprouts growing.

It advanced upon us.

Ellen threw Hasan's burnoose over the head of the swordsman who was about to disembowel her husband. Earth's poet laureate then brought a rock down hard on the top of the burnoose, doubtless collecting much bad karma but not looking too worried about it.

By then Hasan had rejoined our little group, using his hand to parry a sword cut by striking the flat of the blade in an old samuri maneuver I had thought lost to the world forever. Then Hasan, too, had a sword—after another rapid movement—and he was very proficient with it.

We killed or maimed all our guards before the crowd was halfway to us, and Diane, taking a cue from Ellen, lobbed her three magnesium flares across the field and into the mob.

We ran then, Ellen and Red Wig supporting Dos Santos, who was kind of staggery.

But the Kouretes had cut us off and we were running northwards, off at a tangent from our goal.

"We cannot make it, Karagee," called Hasan.

"I know."

". . . Unless you and I delay them while the others go ahead."

"Okay. Where?"

"At the far barbecue pit, where the trees are thick about the path. It is a bottle's neck. They will not be able to hit us all at a time."

"Right!" I turned to the others. "You hear us? Make for the horses! Phil will guide you! Hasan and I will hold them for as long as we can!"

Red Wig turned her head and began to say something.

"Don't argue! Go! You want to live, don't you!?"

They did. They went.

Hasan and I turned, there beside the barbecue pit, and we waited. The others cut back again, going off through the woods, heading toward the village and the paddock. The mob kept right on coming, toward Hasan and me.

The first wave hit us and we began the killing. We were in the V-shaped place where the path disgorged from the woods onto the plain. To our left was a smoldering pit; to our right a thick stand of trees. We killed three, and several more were bleeding when they fell back, paused, then moved to flank us.

We stood back to back then and cut them as they closed.

"If even one has a gun we are dead, Karagee."

"I know."

Another half-man fell to my blade. Hasan sent one, screaming, into the pit.

They were all about us then. A blade slipped in past my guard and cut me on the shoulder. Another nicked my thigh.

"Fall back, thou fools! I say withdraw, thou freaks!"

At that, they did, moving back beyond thrust-range.

The man who had spoken was about five and a half feet tall. His lower jaw moved like that of a puppet's, as though on hinges, and his teeth were like a row of dominoes—all darkstained and clicking as they opened and closed.

"Yea, Procrustes," I heard one say.

"Fetch nets! Snare them alive! Do not close with them! They have cost us too much already!"

Moreby was at his side, and whimpering.

". . . I did not know, m'lord."

"Silence! thou brewer of ill-tasting sloshes! Thou hast cost us a god and many men!"

"Shall we rush?" asked Hasan.

"No, but be ready to cut the nets when they bring them."

"It is not good that they want us alive," he decided.

"We have sent many to Hell, to smooth our way," said I, "and we are standing yet and holding blades. What more?"

"If we rush them we can take two, perhaps four more with us. If we wait, they will net us and we die without them."

"What matters it, once you are dead? Let us wait. So long as we live there is the great peacock-tail of probability, growing from out of the next moment."

"As you say."

And they found nets and cast them. We cut three of them apart before they tangled us in the fourth. They drew them tight and moved in.

I felt my blade wrenched from my grasp, and someone kicked me. It was Moreby.

"Now you will die as very few die," said he.

"Did the others escape?"

"Only for the moment," he said. "We will track them, find them, and bring them back."

I laughed.

"You lose," I said. "They'll make it."

He kicked me again.

"This is how your rule applies?" I asked. "Hasan conquered the Dead Man."

"He cheated. The woman threw a flare."

Procrustes came up beside him as they bound us within the nets.

"Let us take them to the Valley of Sleep," said Moreby, "and there work our wills with them and leave them to be preserved against future feasting."

"It is good," said Procrustes. "Yes, it shall be done."

Hasan must have been working his left arm through the netting all that while, because it shot out a short distance and his nails raked Procrustes' leg.

Procrustes kicked him several times, and me once more for good measure. He rubbed at the scratches on his calf.

"Why did you do that, Hasan?" I asked, after Procrustes turned away and ordered us bound to barbecue stakes for carrying.

"There may still be some meta-cyanide left on my fingernails," he explained.

"How did it get there?"

"From the bullets in my belt, Karagee, which they did not take from me. I coated my nails after I sharpened them today."

"Ah! You scratched the Dead Man at the beginning of your bout . . ."

"Yes, Karagee. Then it was simply a matter of my staying alive until he fell over."

"You are an exemplary assassin, Hasan."

"Thank you, Karagee."

We were bound to the stakes, still netted. Four men, at the order of Procrustes, raised us.

Moreby and Procrustes leading the way, we were borne off through the night.

As we moved along an uneven trail the world changed about us. It's always that way when you approach a Hot Spot. It's like hiking backward through geological eras.

The trees along the way began to vary, more and more. Finally, we were passing up a moist aisle between dark towers with fern-like leaves; and things peered out through them with slitted, yellow eyes. High overhead, the night was a tarp, stretched tentwise across the tree-tops, pricked with faint starmarks, torn with a jagged yellow crescent of a tear. Birdlike cries, ending in snorts, emerged from the great wood. Up further ahead a dark shape crossed the pathway.

As we advanced along the way the trees grew smaller, the spaces between them wider. But they were not like the trees we had left beyond the village. They were twisted (and twisting!) forms, with seaweed swirls of branches, gnarled trunks, and exposed roots which crept, slowly, about the surface of the ground. Tiny invisible things made scratching noises as they scurried from the light of Moreby's electric lantern.

By turning my head I could detect a faint, pulsating glow, just at the border of the visible spectrum. It was coming from up ahead.

A profusion of dark vines appeared underfoot. They writhed whenever one of our bearers stepped on them.

The trees became simple ferns. Then these, too, vanished. Great quantities of shaggy, blood-colored lichens replaced them. They grew over all the rocks. They were faintly luminous.

There were no more animal sounds. There were no sounds at all, save for the panting of our four bearers, and footfalls, and the occasional muffled click as Procrustes' automatic rifle struck a padded rock.

Our bearers wore blades in their belts. Moreby carried several blades, as well as a small pistol.

The trail turned sharply upward. One of our bearers swore. The night-tent was jerked downward at its corners then; it met with the horizon, and it was filled with the hint of a purple haze, fainter than exhaled cigarette-smoke. Slow, very high, and slapping the air like a devilfish coasting on water, the dark form of a spiderbat crossed over the face of the moon.

Procrustes fell.

Moreby helped him to his feet, but Procrustes swayed and leaned upon him.

"What ails you, lord?"

"A sudden dizziness, numbness in my members. . . . Take thou my rifle. It grows heavy."

Hasan chuckled.

Procrustes turned toward Hasan, his puppet-jaw dropping open.

Then he dropped, too.

Moreby had just taken the rifle and his hands

were full. The guards set us down, rather urgently, and rushed to Procrustes' side.

"Hast thou any water?" he asked, and he closed his eyes.

He did not open them again.

Moreby listened to his chest, held the feathery part of his wand beneath his nostrils.

"He is dead," he finally announced.

"Dead?"

The bearer who was covered with scales began to weep.

"He wiss good," he sobbed. "He wiss a great war shief. What will we do now?"

"He is dead," Moreby repeated, "and I am your leader until a new war chief is declared. Wrap him in your cloaks. Leave him on that flat rock up ahead. No animals come here, so he will not be molested. We will recover him on the way back. Now, though, we must have our vengeance on these two." He gestured with his wand. "The Valley of Sleep is near at hand. You have taken the pills I gave you?"

"Yes."

"Yes."

"Yes."

"Yiss."

"Very good. Take your cloaks now and wrap him."

They did this, and soon we were raised again and borne to the top of a ridge from which a trail ran down into a fluorescent, pock-blasted pit. The great rocks of the place seemed almost to be burning.

"This," I said to Hasan, "was described to me by my son as the place where the thread of my life lies across a burning stone. He saw me as threatened by the Dead Man, but the fates thought twice and gave that menace onto you. Back when I was but a dream in the mind of Death, this site was appointed as one of the places where I might die."

"To fall from Shinvat is to roast," said Hasan.

The carried us down into the fissure, dropped us on the rocks.

Moreby released the safety catch on the rifle and stepped back.

"Release the Greek and tie him to that column." He gestured with the weapon.

They did this, binding my hands and feet securely. The rock was smooth, damp, killing without indication.

They did the same to Hasan, about eight feet to my right.

Moreby had set down the lantern so that it cast a yellow semicircle about us. The four Kouretes were demon statues at his side.

He smiled. He leaned the rifle against the rocky wall behind him.

"This is the Valley of Sleep," he told us. "Those who sleep here do not awaken. It keeps the meat preserved, however, providing us against the lean years. Before we leave you, though—" His eyes turned to me. "Do you see where I have set the rifle?"

I did not answer him.

"I believe your entrails will stretch that far, Commissioner. At any rate, I intend to find out." He drew a dagger from his belt and advanced upon me. The four half-men moved with him. "Who do you think has more guts?" he asked. "You or the Arab?"

Neither of us replied.

"You shall both get to see for yourselves," he said through his teeth. "First you!"

He jerked my shirt free and cut it down the front. He rotated the blade in a slow significant circle about two inches away from my stomach, all the while studying my face.

"You are afraid," he said. "Your face does not show it yet, but it will."

Then: "Look at me! I am going to put the blade in very slowly. I am going to dine on you one day. What do you think of that?"

I laughed. It was suddenly worth laughing at.

His face twisted, then it straightened into a momentary look of puzzlement.

"Has the fear driven you mad, Commissioner?"

"Feathers or lead?" I asked him.

He knew what it meant. He started to say something, and then he heard a pebble click about twelve feet away. His head snapped in that direction.

He spent the last second of his life screaming, as the force of Bortan's leap pulped him against the ground, before his head was snatched from his shoulders.

My hellhound had arrived.

The Kouretes screamed, for his eyes are glowing coals and his teeth are buzzsaws. His head is as high above the ground as a tall man's. Although they seized their blades and struck at him, his sides are as the sides of an armadillo. A quarter ton of dog, my Bortan . . . he is not exactly the kind Albert Payson Terhune wrote about.

He worked for the better part of a minute, and when he was finished they were all in pieces and none of them alive.

"What is it?" asked Hasan.

"A puppy I found in a sack, washed up on the beach, too tough to drown—my dog," said I, "Bortan."

There was a small gash in the softer part of his shoulder. He had not gotten it in the fight.

"He sought us first in the village," I said, "and they tried to stop him. Many Kouretes have died this day."

He trotted up and licked my face. He wagged his tail, made dog-noises, wriggled like a puppy, and ran in small circles. He sprang toward me and licked my face again. Then he was off cavorting once more, treading on pieces of Kouretes.

"It is good for a man to have a dog," said Hasan. "I have always been fond of dogs."

Bortan was sniffing him as he said it.

"You've come back, you dirty old hound," I told him. "Don't you know that dogs are extinct?"

He wagged his tail, came up to me again, licked my hand.

"I'm sorry that I can't scratch your ears. You know that I'd like to, though, don't you?"

He wagged his tail.

I opened and closed my right hand within its bonds. I turned my head that way as I did it. Bortan watched, his nostrils moist and quivering.

"Hands, Bortan. I need hands to free me. Hands to loosen my bonds. You must fetch them, Bortan, and bring them here."

He picked up an arm that was lying on the

ground and he deposited it at my feet. He looked up then and wagged his tail.

"No, Bortan. *Live* hands. Friendly hands. Hands to untie me. You understand, don't you?"

He licked my hand.

"Go and find hands to free me. Still attached and living. The hands of friends. Now, quickly! Go!"

He turned and walked away, paused, looked back once, then mounted the trail.

"Does he understand?" asked Hasan.

"I think so," I told him. "His is not an ordinary dog brain, and he has had many many more years than even the lifetime of a man in which to learn understanding."

"Then let us hope he finds someone quickly, before we sleep."

"Yes."

We hung there and the night was cold.

We waited for a long time. Finally, we lost track of time.

Our muscles were cramped and aching. We were covered with the dried blood of countless little wounds. We were all over bruises. We were groggy from fatigue, from lack of sleep.

We hung there, the ropes cutting into us.

"Do you think they will make it to your village?"

"We gave them a good start. I think they have a decent chance."

"It is always difficult to work with you, Karagee."

"I know. I have noticed this same thing myself."

". . . Like the summer we rotted in the dungeons of Corsica."

"Aye."

". . . Or our march to the Chicago Station, after we had lost all our equipment in Ohio."

"Yes, that was a bad year."

"You are *always* in trouble, though, Karagee. 'Born to knot the tiger's tail,' " he said; "that is the saying for people such as you. They are difficult to be with. Myself, I love the quiet and the shade, a book of poems, my pipe—"

"Hush! I hear something!"

There was a clatter of hooves.

A satyr appeared beyond the cockeyed angle of the light from the fallen lantern. He moved nervously, his eyes going from me to Hasan and back again, and up, down, around, and past us.

"Help us, little horny one," said I, in Greek.

He advanced carefully. He saw the blood, the mangled Kouretes.

He turned as if to flee.

"Come back! I need you! It is I, the player of the pipes."

He stopped and turned again, his nostrils quivering, flaring and falling. His pointed ears twitched.

He came back, a pained expression on his near-human face as he passed through the place of gore.

"The blade. At my feet," I said, gesturing with my eyes. "Pick it up."

He did not seem to like the notion of touching anything man-made, especially a weapon.

I whistled the last lines of my last tune.

It's late, it's late, so late. . . .

His eyes grew moist. He wiped at them with the backs of his shaggy wrists.

"Pick up the blade and cut my bonds. Pick it up.

—Not that way, you'll cut yourself. The other end.
—Yes."

He picked it up properly and looked at me. I moved my right hand.

"The ropes. Cut them."

He did. It took him twenty minutes and left me wearing a bracelet of blood. I had to keep moving my hand to keep him from slashing an artery. But he freed it and looked at me expectantly.

"Now give me the knife and I'll take care of the rest."

He placed the blade in my extended hand.

I took it. Seconds later I was free. Then I freed Hasan.

When I turned again the satyr was gone. I heard the sound of frantic hoofbeats in the distance.

"The Devil has forgiven me," said Hasan.

We went far away from the Hot Spot as fast as we could, skirting the Kourete village and continuing northward until we came upon a trail that I recognized as the road to Volos. Whether Bortan had found the satyr and had somehow conned him into coming to us, or whether the creature had spotted us himself and remembered me, was something of which I couldn't be sure. Bortan had not returned, though, so I had a feeling it was the latter case.

The closest friendly town was Volos, a probable twenty-five kilometers to the east. If Bortan had gone there, where he would be recognized by many of my relatives, it would still be a long while before his return. My sending him after help had been a last-ditch sort of thing. If he'd tried elsewhere than Volos, then I'd no idea when he'd be back. He'd find my trail though, and he'd follow it again. We pushed on, putting as much road as possible behind us.

After about ten kilo we were staggering. We knew that we couldn't make it much further without rest, so we kept our eyes open for a possible safe sleep-site.

Finally, I recognized a steep, rocky hill where I had herded sheep as a boy. The small shepherd's cave, three-quarters of the way up the slope, was dry and vacant. The wooden facade that faced it was fallen to decay, but it still functioned.

We pulled some clean grass for bedding, secured the door, and stretched out within. In a moment, Hasan was snoring. My mind spun for a second before it drifted, and in that second I knew that of all pleasures—a drink of cold water when you are thirsty, liquor when you are not, sex, a cigarette after many days without one—there is none of them can compare with sleep.

Sleep is best. . . .

I might say that if our party had taken the long way from Lamia to Volos—the coastal road—the whole thing might never have happened the way that it did, and Phil might be alive today. But I can't really judge all that occurred in this case; even now, looking back, I can't say how I'd rearrange events if it were all to be done over again. The forces of final disruption were already goosestepping amidst the ruins, arms upraised. . . .

We made it to Volos the following afternoon, and on up Mount Pelion to Portaria. Across a deep ravine lay Makrynitsa.

We crossed over and found the others.

Phil had guided them to Makrynitsa, asked for a bottle of wine and his copy of *Prometheus Unbound,* and had sat up with the two, well into the evening.

In the morning, Diane had found him smiling, and cold.

I built him a pyre amidst the cedars near the ruined Episcopi, because he did not want to be buried. I heaped it with incense, with aromatic herbs, and it was twice the height of a man. That night it would burn and I would say goodbye to another friend. It seems, looking back, that my life has mainly been a series of arrivals and departures. I say "hello." I say "goodbye." Only the Earth endures. . . .

Hell.

So I walked with the group that afternoon, out to Pagasae, the port of ancient Iolkos, set on the promontory opposite Volos. We stood in the shade of the almond trees on the hill that gives good vantage to both seascape and rocky ridge.

"It was from here that the Argonauts set sail on their quest for the Golden Fleece," I told no one in particular.

"Who all were they?" asked Ellen. "I read the story in school, but I forget."

"There was Herakles and Theseus and Orpheus the singer, and Asclepius, and the sons of the North Wind, and Jason, the captain, who was a pupil of the centaur, Cheiron—whose cave, incidentally, is up near the summit of Mount Pelion, there."

"Really?"

"I'll show it to you sometime."

"All right."

"The gods and the titans battled near here also," said Diane, coming up on my other side. "Did the titans not uproot Mount Pelion and pile it atop Ossa in an attempt to scale Olympus?"

"So goes the telling. But the gods were kind and restored the scenery after the bloody battle."

"A sail," said Hasan, gesturing with a half-peeled orange in his hand.

I looked out over the waters and there was a tiny blip on the horizon.

"Yes; this place is still used as a port."

"Perhaps it is a shipload of heroes," said Ellen, "returning with some more fleece. What will they do with all that fleece, anyhow?"

"It's not the fleece that's important," said Red Wig, "it's the getting of it. Every good story-teller used to know that. The womenfolk can always make stunning garments from fleeces. They're used to picking up the remains after quests."

"It wouldn't match your hair, dear."

"Yours either, child."

"That can be changed. Not so easily as yours, of course. . . ."

"Across the way," said I, in a loud voice, "is a ruined Byzantine church—the Episcopi—which I've scheduled for restoration in another two years. It is the traditional site of the wedding feast of Peleus, also one of the Argonauts, and the sea-nymph Thetis. Perhaps you've heard the story of that feast? Everyone was invited but the goddess of discord, and she came anyhow and tossed down a golden apple marked 'For the Fairest.' Lord Paris judged it the property of Aphrodite, and the fate of Troy was sealed. The last time anyone saw Paris, he was none too happy. Ah, decisions! Like I've often said, this land is lousy with myth."

"How long will we be here?" asked Ellen.

"I'd like a couple more days in Makrynitsa," I said, "then we'll head northwards. Say about a week more in Greece, and then we'll move on to Rome."

"No," said Myshtigo, who had been sitting on a rock and talking to his machine, as he stared out over the waters. "No, the tour is finished. This is the last stop."

"How come?"

"I'm satisfied and I'm going home now."

"What about your book?"

"I've got my story."

"What kind of story?"

"I'll send you an autographed copy when it's finished. My time is precious, and I have all the material I want now. All that I'll need, anyhow. I called the Port this morning, and they are sending me a Skimmer tonight. You people go ahead and do whatever you want, but I'm finished."

"Is something wrong?"

"No, nothing is wrong, but it's time that I left. I have much to do."

He rose to his feet and stretched.

"I have some packing to take care of, so I'll be going back now. You *do* have a beautiful country here, Conrad, despite.—I'll see you all at dinnertime."

He turned and headed down the hill.

I walked a few steps in his direction, watching him go.

"I wonder what prompted that?" I thought aloud.

There was a footfall.

"He is dying," said George, softly.

* * *

My son Jason, who had preceded us by several days, was gone. Neighbors told of his departure for Hades on the previous evening. The patriarch had been carried off on the back of a fire-eyed hellhound who had knocked down the door of his dwelling place and borne him off through the night. My relatives all wanted me to come to dinner. Dos Santos was still resting; George had treated his wounds and had not deemed it necessary to ship him to the hospital in Athens.

It's always nice to come home.

I walked down to the Square and spent the afternoon talking to my descendants. Would I tell them of Taler, of Haiti, of Athens? Aye. I would, I did. Would they tell me of the past two decades in Makrynitsa? Ditto.

I took some flowers to the graveyard then, stayed awhile, and went to Jason's home and repaired his door with some tools I found in the shed. Then I came upon a bottle of wine and drank it all. And I smoked a cigar. I made me a pot of coffee, too, and I drank all of that.

I still felt depressed.

I didn't know what was coming off.

George knew his diseases, though, and he said the Vegan showed unmistakable symptoms of a neurological disorder of the e.t. variety. Incurable. Invariably fatal.

And even Hasan couldn't take credit for it. "Etiology unknown" was George's diagnosis.

So everything was revised.

George had known about Myshtigo since the reception.—What had set him on the track?

—Phil had asked him to observe the Vegan for signs of a fatal disease.

Why?

Well, he hadn't said why, and I couldn't go ask him at the moment.

I had me a problem.

Myshtigo had either finished his job or he hadn't enough time left to do it. He *said* he'd finished it. If he hadn't, then I'd been protecting a dead man all the while, to no end. If he had, then I needed to know the results, so that I could make a very fast decision concerning what remained of his lifespan.

Dinner was no help. Myshtigo had said all he cared to say, and he ignored or parried our questions. So, as soon as we'd had our coffee, Red Wig and I stepped outside for a cigarette.

"What's happened?" she asked.

"I don't know. I thought maybe you did."

"No. What now?"

"You tell me."

"Kill him?"

"Perhaps yes. First though, why?"

"He's finished it."

"What? Just *what* has he finished?"

"How should I know?"

"Damn it! *I* have to! I like to know why I'm killing somebody. I'm funny that way."

"Funny? Very. Obvious, isn't it? The Vegans want to buy in again, Earthside. He's going back to give them a report on the sites they're interested in."

"They why didn't he visit them all? Why cut it short after Egypt and Greece? Sand, rocks, jungles, and assorted monsters—that's all he saw. Hardly makes for an encouraging appraisal."

"Then he's scared, is why, and lucky he's alive.

He could have been eaten by a boadile or Kourete. He's running."

"Good. Then let him run. Let him hand in a bad report."

"He can't, though. If they *do* want in, they won't buy anything that sketchy. They'll just send somebody else—somebody tougher—to finish it. If we kill Myshtigo they'll know we're still for real, still protesting, still tough ourselves."

". . . And he's not afraid for his life," I mused.

"No? What, then?"

"I don't know. I have to find out, though."

"How?"

"I think I'll ask him."

"You are a lunatic." She turned away.

"My way, or not at all," I said.

"*Any* way, then. It doesn't matter. We've already lost."

I took her by the shoulders and kissed her neck. "Not yet. You'll see."

She stood stiffly.

"Go home," she said; "it's late. It's too late."

I did that. I went back to Iakov Korones' big old place, where Myshtigo and I were both quartered, and where Phil had been staying.

I stopped there in the deathroom, in the place where Phil had last slept. His *Prometheus Unbound* was still on the writing table, set down beside an empty bottle. He had spoken of his own passing when he'd called me in Egypt, and he had suffered an attack, had been through a lot. It seemed he'd leave a message for an old friend then, on a matter like this.

So I opened Percy B's dud epic and looked within.

It was written on the blank pages at the end of the book, in Greek. Not modern Greek, though. Classical.

It went something like this:

Dear friend, although I abhor writing anything I cannot rewrite, I feel I had best tend to this with dispatch. I am unwell. George wants me to skim to Athens. I will, too, in the morning. First, though, regarding the matter at hand—

Get the Vegan off the Earth, alive, at any cost.

It is important.

It is the most important thing in the world.

I was afraid to tell you before, because I thought Myshtigo might be a telepath. That is why I did not go along for the entire journey, though I should dearly have loved to do so. That is why I pretended to hate him, so that I could stay away from him as much as possible. It was only after I managed to confirm the fact that he was not telepathic that I elected to join you.

I suspected, what with Dos Santos, Diane, and Hasan, and the Radpol might be out for his blood. If he was a telepath, I figured he would learn of this quickly and do whatever needed to be done to assure his safety. If he was not a telepath, I still had great faith in your ability to defend him against almost anything, Hasan included. But I did not want him apprised of my knowledge. I did *try to warn you, though, if you recall.*

*Tatram Yshtigo, his grandfather, is one of the finest, most noble creatures alive. He is a philosopher, a great writer, an altruistic administrator of services to the public. I became acquainted with him during my stay on Taler, thirty-some years ago, and we later became close friends. We have been in communication ever since that time, and that far back, even, was I advised by him of the Vegan Combine's plans regarding the disposition of Earth. I was also sworn to secrecy. Even Cort cannot know that I am aware. The old man *would lose face, disastrously, if this thing came out ahead of time.*

The Vegans are in a very embarrassing position. Our expatriate countrymen have forced their own economic and cultural dependence upon Vega. The Vegans were made aware —quite vividly!—during the days of the Radpol Rebellion, of the fact that there is an indigenous population possessing a strong organization of its own and desiring the restoration of our planet. The Vegans too would like to see this happen. They do not want the Earth. Whatever for? If they want to exploit Earthfolk, they have more of them on Taler than we do here on Earth—and they're not doing it; not massively or maliciously, at any rate. Our ex-pop has elected what labor exploitation it does undergo in preference to returning here. What does this indicate? Returnism is a dead issue. No one is coming back. That is why I quit the movement. Why you did too, I believe. The Vegans would like to get the home world problem off their hands. Sure, they want to visit it. It is instructive, sobering, humbling, and downright frightening for them to come here and see what can be done to a world.

What needed to be done was for them to find a way around our ex-pop gov on Taler. The Talerites were not anxious to give up their only claim for taxes and existence: the Office.

After much negotiation, though, and much economic suasion, including the offer of full Vegan citizenship to our ex-pop, it appeared that a means had been found. The implementation of the plan was given into the hands of the Shtigo gens, Tatram in especial.

He finally found a way, he believed, of returning the Earth proper to an autonomous position and preserving its cultural integrity. That is why he sent his grandson, Cort, to do his 'survey.' Cort is a strange creature; his real talent is acting (all the Shtigo are quite gifted), and he loves to pose. I believe that he wanted to play the part of an alien very badly, and I am certain that he has carried it with skill and efficiency. (Tatram also advised me that it would be Cort's last *role. He is dying of* drinfan, *which is incurable; also, I believe it is the reason he was chosen.)*

Believe me, Konstantin Karaghiosis Korones Nomikos (and all the others which I do not know), Conrad, when I say that he was not surveying real estate: No.

But allow me one last Bryonic gesture. Take my word that he must live, and let me keep my promise and my secret. You will not regret it, when you know all.

I am sorry that I never got to finish your elegy, and damn you for keeping my Lara, that time in Kerch!—PHIL

Very well then, I decided—life, not death, for the Vegan. Phil had spoken and I did not doubt his words.

I went back to Mikar Korones' dinner table and stayed with Myshtigo until he was ready to leave. I accompanied him back to Iakov Korones' and watched him pack some final items. We exchanged maybe six words during this time.

His belongings we carried out to the place where the Skimmer would land, in front of the house. Before the others (including Hasan) came up to bid him goodbye, he turned to me and said, "Tell me, Conrad, why are you tearing down the pyramid?"

"To needle Vega," I said. "To let you know that if you want this place and you do manage to take it away from us, you'll get it in worse shape than it was after the Three Days. There wouldn't be anything left to look at. We'd burn the rest of our history. Not even a scrap for you guys."

The air escaping from the bottom of his lungs came out with a high-pitched whine—the Vegan equivalent of a sigh.

"Commendable, I suppose," he said, "but I did so want to see it. Do you think you could ever get it back together again? Soon, perhaps?"

"What do you think?"

"I noticed your men marking many of the pieces."

I shrugged.

"I have only one serious question, then—about your fondness for destruction . . ." he stated.

"What is that?"

"Is it *really* art?"

"Go to hell."

Then the others came up. I shook my head slowly at Diane and seized Hasan's wrist long enough to tear away a tiny needle he'd taped to the palm of his hand. I let him shake hands with the Vegan too, then, briefly.

The Skimmer buzzed down out of the darkening sky, and I saw Myshtigo aboard, loaded his baggage personally, and closed the door myself.

It took off without incident and was gone in a matter of moments.

End of a nothing jaunt.

I went back inside and changed my clothing.

It was time to burn a friend.

Heaped high into the night, my ziggurat of logs bore what remained of the poet, my friend. I kindled a torch and put out the electric lantern. Hasan stood at my side. He had helped bear the corpse to the cart and had taken over the reins. I had built the pyre on the cypress-filled hill above

Volos, near the ruins of that church I mentioned earlier. The waters of the bay were calm. The sky was clear and the stars were bright.

Dos Santos, who did not approve of cremation, had decided not to attend, saying that his wounds were troubling him. Diane had elected to remain with him back in Makrynitsa. She had not spoken to me since our last conversation.

Ellen and George were seated on the bed of the cart, which was backed beneath a large cypress, and they were holding hands. They were the only others present. Phil would not have liked my relatives wailing their dirges about him. He'd once said he wanted something big, bright, fast, and without music.

I applied the torch to a corner of the pyre. The flame bit, slowly, began to chew at the wood. Hasan started another torch going, stuck it into the ground, stepped back, and watched.

As the flames ate their way upwards I prayed the old prayers and poured out wine upon the ground. I heaped aromatic herbs onto the blaze. Then I, too, stepped back.

"'. . . Whatever you were, death has taken you, too,'" I told him. "'You have gone to see the moist flower open along Acheron, among Hell's shadows darting fitfully.' Had you died young, your passing would have been mourned as the destruction of a great talent before its fulfillment. But you lived and they cannot say that now. Some choose a short and supernal life before the walls of their Troy, others a long and less troubled one. And who is to say which is the better? The gods did keep their promise of immortal fame to Achilleus, by inspiring the poet to sing him an immortal paean. But is he the happier for it, being now as dead as yourself? *I* cannot judge, old friend. Lesser bard, I remember some of the words you, too, wrote of the mightiest of the Argives, and of the time of hard-hurled deaths: 'Bleak disappointments rage this coming-together place: Menace of sighs in a jeopardy of time. . . . But the ashes do not burn backward to timber. Flame's invisible music shapes the air to heat, but the day is no longer.' Fare thee well, Phillip Graver. May the Lords Phoebus and Dionysius, who do love and kill their poets, commend thee to their dark brother Hades. And may his Persephone, Queen of the Night, look with favor upon thee and grant thee high stead in Elysium. Goodbye."

The flames had almost reached the top.

I saw Jason then, standing beside the cart, Bortan seated by his side. I backed away further. Bortan came to me and sat down at my right. He licked my hand, once.

"Mighty hunter, we have lost us another,' I said.

He nodded his great head.

The flames reached the top and began to nibble at the night. The air was filled with sweet aromas and the sound of fire.

Jason approached.

"Father," he said, "he bore me to the place of burning rocks, but you were already escaped."

I nodded.

"A no-man friend freed us from that place. Before that, this man Hasan destroyed the Dead Man. So your dreams have thus far proved both right and wrong."

"*He* is the yellow-eyed warrior of my vision," he said.

"I know, but that part too is past."

"What of the Black Beast?"

"Not a snort nor a snuffle."

"Good."

We watched for a long, long time, as the light retreated into itself. At several points, Bortan's ears pricked forward and his nostrils dilated. George and Ellen had not moved. Hasan was a strange-eyed watcher, without expression.

"What will you do now, Hasan?" I asked.

"Go again to Mount Sindjar," he said, "for awhile."

"And then?"

He shrugged. "Howsoever it is written," he replied.

And a fearsome noise came upon us then, like the groans of an idiot giant, and the sound of splintering trees accompanied it.

Bortan leaped to his feet and howled. The donkeys who had drawn the cart shifted uneasily. One of them made a brief, braying noise.

Jason clutched the sharpened staff which he had picked from the heap of kindling, and he stiffened.

It burst in upon us then, there in the clearing. Big, and ugly, and everything it had ever been called.

The Eater of Men. . . .

The Shaker of the Earth. . . .

The Mighty, Foul One. . . .

The Black Beast of Thessaly.

Finally, someone could say what it really was. If they got away to say it, that is.

It must have been drawn to us by the odor of burning flesh.

And it *was* big. The size of an elephant, at least.

What was Herakles' fourth labor?

The wild boar of Arcadia, that's what.

I suddenly wished Herk was still around to help.

A big pig. . . . A razorback, with tusks the length of a man's arm. . . . Little pig eyes, black, and rolling in the firelight, wildly. . . .

It knocked down trees as it came. . . .

It squealed, though, as Hasan drew a burning brand from the blaze and drove it, fire-end forward, into its snout, and then spun away.

It swerved, too, which gave me time to snatch Jason's staff.

I ran forward and caught it in the left eye with it.

It swerved again then, and squealed like a leaky boiler.

. . . And Bortan was upon it, tearing at its shoulder.

Neither of my two thrusts at its throat did more than superficial damage. It wrestled, shoulder against fang, and finally shook itself free of Bortan's grip.

Hasan was at my side by then, waving another firebrand.

It charged us.

From somewhere off to the side George emptied a machine-pistol into it. Hasan hurled the torch. Bortan leapt again, this time from its blind side.

. . . And these things caused it to swerve once more in its charge, crashing into the now empty cart and killing both donkeys.

I ran against it then, thrusting the staff up under its left front leg.

The staff broke in two.

Bortan kept biting, and his snarl was a steady thunder. Whenever it slashed at him with its tusks he relinquished his grip, danced away, and moved in again to worry it.

I am sure that my needle-point deathlance of steel would not have broken. It had been aboard the *Vanitie,* though. . . .

Hasan and I circled it with the sharpest and most stake-like of the kindling we could find. We kept jabbing, to keep it turning in a circle. Bortan kept trying for its throat, but the great snouted head stayed low, and the one eye rolled and the other bled, and the tusks slashed back and forth and up and down like swords. Cloven hooves the size of bread-loaves tore great holes in the ground as it turned, counterclockwise, trying to kill us all, there in the orange and dancing flamelight.

Finally, it stopped and turned—suddenly, for something that big—and its shoulders struck Bortan in the side and hurled him ten or twelve feet past me. Hasan hit it across the back with his stick and I drove in toward the other eye, but missed.

Then it moved toward Bortan, who was still regaining his feet—its head held low, tusks gleaming.

I threw my staff and leapt as it moved in on my dog. It had already dropped its head for the death blow.

I caught both tusks as the head descended almost to the ground. Nothing could hold back that scooping slash, I realized, as I bore down upon it with all my strength.

But I tried, and maybe I succeeded, somehow, for a second. . . .

At least, as I was thrown through the air, my hands torn and bleeding, I saw that Bortan had managed to get back out of the way.

I was dazed by the fall, for I had been thrown far and high; and I heard a great pig-mad squealing. Hasan screamed and Bortan roared out his great-throated battle-challenge once more.

. . . And the hot red lightning of Zeus descended twice from the heavens.

. . . And all was still.

I climbed back, slowly, to my feet.

Hasan was standing by the blazing pyre, a flaming stake still upraised in spear-throwing position.

Bortan was sniffing at the quivering mountain of flesh.

Cassandra was standing beneath the cypress beside a dead donkey, her back against the trunk of the tree, wearing leather trousers, a blue woolen shirt, a faint smile, and my still-smoking elephant gun.

"Cassandra!"

She dropped the gun and looked very pale. But I had her in my arms almost before it hit the ground.

"I'll ask you a lot of things later," I said. "Not now. Nothing now. Let's just sit here beneath this tree and watch the fire burn."

And we did.

A month later, Dos Santos was ousted from the Radpol. He and Diane have not been heard of since. Rumor has it that they gave up on Returnism, moved to Taler, and are living there now. I hope it's not true, what with the affairs of these past five days. I never did know the full story on Red Wig, and I guess I never will. If you trust a person, really trust him I mean, and you care for him, as she might have cared for me, it would seem you'd stick around to see whether he was right or wrong on your final big disagreement. She didn't, though, and I wonder if she regrets it now.

I don't really think I'll ever see her again.

Slightly after the Radpol shakeup, Hasan returned from Mount Sindjar, stayed awhile at the Port, then purchased a small ship and put out to sea early one morning, without even saying goodbye or giving any indication as to his destination. It was assumed he'd found new employment somewhere. There was a hurricane, though, several days later, and I heard rumors in Trinidad to the effect that he had been washed up on the coast of Brazil and met with his death at the hands of the fierce tribesmen who dwell there. I tried but was unable to verify this story.

However, two months later, Ricardo Bonaventura, Chairman of the Alliance Against Progress, a Radpol splinter group which had fallen into disfavor with Athens, died of apoplexy during a Party function. There were some murmurings of Divban rabbit-venon in the anchovies (an exceedingly lethal combination, George assures me), and the following day the new Captain of the Palace Guard vanished mysteriously, along with a Skimmer and the minutes of the last three secret sessions of the AAP (not to mention the contents of a small wallsafe). He was said to have been a big-, yellow-eyed man, with a slightly Eastern cast to his features.

Jason is still herding his many-legged sheep in the high places, up where the fingers of Aurora come first to smear the sky with roses, and doubtless he is corrupting youth with his song.

Ellen is pregnant again, all delicate and big-waisted, and won't talk to anybody but George. George wants to try some fancy embryosurgery, now, before it's too late, and make his next kid a water-breather as well as an air-breather, because of all that great big virgin frontier down underneath the ocean, where his descendants can pioneer, and him be father to a new race and write an interesting book on the subject, and all that. Ellen is not too hot on the idea, though, so I have a hunch the oceans will remain virgin a little longer.

Oh yes, I did take George to Capistrano some time ago, to watch the spiderbats return. It was real impressive—them darkening the sky with their flight, nesting about the ruins the way they do, eating the wild pigs, leaving green droppings all over the streets. Lorel has hours and hours of it in tri-dee color, and he shows it at every Office party. It's sort of a historical document, spiderbats being on the way out now. True to his word, George started a *slishi* plague among them, and they're dropping like flies these days. Just the other week one dropped down in the middle of the street with a big *splatt!* as I was on my way to Mama Julie's with a bottle of rum and a box of chocolates. It was quite dead when it hit. The *slishi* are very insidious. The poor spiderbat doesn't know what's happening; he's flying along happily, looking for someone to eat, and then *zock!* it hits him, and he falls into the middle of a garden party or sombody's swimming pool.

I've decided to retain the Office for the time being. I'll set up some kind of parliament after I've whipped up an opposition party to the Radpol—Indreb, or something like that maybe: like Independent Rebuilders, or such.

Good old final forces of disruption . . . we needed them down here amid the ruins.

And Cassandra—my princess, my angel, my lovely lady—she even likes me without my fungus. That night in the Valley of Sleep did it in.

She, of course, had been the shipload of heroes Hasan had seen that day back at Pagasea. No golden fleece, though, just my gunrack and such. It had been the *Golden Vanitie*, which I'd built by hand, me, stout enough, I was pleased to learn, to take even the *tsunami* that followed that 9.6 Richter thing. She'd been out sailing in it at the time the bottom fell out of Kos. Afterwards, she'd set sail for Volos because she knew Makrynitsa was full of my relatives. Oh, good thing—that she had had this *feeling* that there was danger and had carried the heavy artillery ashore with her. (Good thing, too, that she knew how to use it.) I'll have to learn to take her premonitions more seriously.

I've purchased a quiet villa on the end of Haiti opposite from the Port. It's only about fifteen minutes' skimming time from there, and it has a big beach and lots of jungle all around it. I have to have some distance, like the whole island, between me and civilization, because I have this, well—hunting—problem. The other day, when the attorneys dropped around, they didn't understand the sign: BEWARE THE DOG. They do now. The one who's in traction won't sue for damages, and George will have him as good as new in no time. The others were not so severely taken.

Good thing I was nearby, though.

So here I am, in an unusual position, as usual.

The entire planet Earth was purchased from the Talerite government, purchased by the large and wealthy Shtigo gens. The preponderance of expatriates wanted Vegan citizenship anyhow, rather than remaining under the Talerite exgov and working in the Combine as registered aliens. This has been coming for a long time, so the disposal of the Earth became mainly a matter of finding the best buyer—because our exile regime lost its only other cause for existence the minute the citizenship thing went through. They could justify themselves while there were still Earthmen out there, but now they're all Vegans and can't vote for them, and *we're* sure not going to, down here.

Hence, the sale of a lot of real estate—and the only bidder was the Shtigo gens.

Wise old Tatram saw that the Shtigo gens did not own Earth, though. The entire purchase was made in the name of his grandson, the late Cort Myshtigo.

And Myshtigo left this distribution-desire, or last will and testament, Vegan-style . . .

. . . in which I was named.

I've, uh, inherited a planet.

The Earth, to be exact.

Well—

Hell, I don't want the thing. I mean, sure I'm stuck with it for awhile, but I'll work something out.

It was that infernal Vite-Stats machine, and four other big think-tanks that old Tatram used. He was looking for a local administrator to hold the earth in fief and set up a resident representative government, and then to surrender ownership on a fairly simple residency basis once things got rolling. He wanted somebody who'd been around awhile, was qualified as an administrator, and who wouldn't want to keep the place for his very own.

Among others, it gave him one of my names, then another, the second as a "possibly still living." Then my personnel file was checked, and more stuff on the other guy, and pretty soon the machine had turned up a few more names, all of them mine. It began picking up discrepancies and peculair similarities, kept kapocketting, and gave out more puzzling answers.

Before long, Tatram decided I had better be "surveyed."

Cort came to write a book.

He really wanted to see if I was Good, Honest, Noble, Pure, Loyal, Faithful, Trustworthy, Selfless, Kind, Cheerful, Dependable, and Without Personal Ambition.

Which means he was a cockeyed lunatic, because he said, "Yes, he's all that."

I sure fooled him.

Maybe he was right about the lack of personal ambition, though. I am pretty damn lazy, and am not at all anxious to acquire the headaches I see as springing up out of the tormented Earth and blackjacking me daily.

However, I am willing to make certain concessions so far as personal comfort is concerned. I'll probably cut myself back to a six-month vacation.

One of the attorneys (not the one in traction—the one with the sling) delivered me a note from the Blue One. It said, in part:

Dear Whatever-the-Blazes-Your-Name-Is,

It is most unsettling to begin a letter this way, so I'll respect your wishes and call you Conrad.

"Conrad," by now you are aware of the true nature of my visit. I feel I have made a good choice in naming you as heir to the property commonly referred to as Earth. Your affection

for it cannot be gainsaid; as Karaghiosis you inspired men to bleed in its defense; you are restoring its monuments, preserving its works of art (and as one stipulation of my will, by the way, I insist that you put back the Great Pyramid!), and your ingenuity as well as your toughness, both physical and mental, is singularly amazing.

You also appear to be the closest thing to an immortal overseer available (I'd give a lot to know your real age), and this, together with your high survival potential, makes you, really, the only candidate. If your mutation every does begin to fail you, there is always the S-S series to continue linking the great chain of your days. (I could have said "forging," but it would not have been polite, inasmuch as I know you are an accomplished forger.—All those old records! You drove poor Vite-Stats half-mad with discrepancies. It is now programmed never to accept another Greek birth certificate as proof of age!)

I commend the Earth into the hands of the Kallikanzaros. According to legend, this would be a grave mistake. However, I am willing to gamble that you are even a kallikanzaros under false pretenses. You destroy only what you mean to rebuild. Probably you are Great Pan, who only pretended to die. Whatever, you will have sufficient funds and a supply of heavy equipment which will be sent this year —and lots of forms for requisitioning more from the Shtigo Foundation. So go thou and be thou fruitful and multiply, and reinherit the Earth. The gens will be around watching. Cry out if you need help, and help will be forthcoming.

I don't have time to write you a book. Sorry. Here is my autograph, anyhow:

—CORT MYSHTIGO

P.S. I still dunno if it's art. Go to hell yourself.

That is the gist of it.

Pan?

Machines don't talk that way, do they?

I hope not, anyhow. . . .

The Earth is a wild inhabitation. It is a tough and rocky place. The rubbish will have to be cleared, section by section, before some anti-rubbish can be put up.

Which means work, lots of it.

Which means I'll need all the Office facilities as well as the Radpol organization, to begin with.

Right now I'm deciding whether or not to discontinue the ruin-tours. I think I'll let them go on, because for once we'll have something good to show. There is that certain element of human curiosity which demands that one halt in his course and peer through a hole in any fence behind which construction work is going on.

We have money now, and we own our own property again, and that makes a big difference. Maybe even Returnism isn't completely dead. If there is a vital program to revive the Earth, we may draw back some of the ex-pop, may snag some of the new tourists.

Or, if they all want to remain Vegans, they can do that, too. We'd like them, but we don't need them. Our Outbound immigration will be dropping off, I feel, once people know they can get ahead here; and our population will increase more than just geometrically, what with the prolonged fertility period brought on by the now quite expensive S-S series. I intend to socialize S-S completely. I'll do it by putting George in charge of a Public Health program, featuring mainland clinics and offering S-S all over the place.

We'll make out. I'm tired of being a gravekeeper, and I don't really want to spend from now till

Easter cutting through the Tree of the World, even if I am a Darkborn with a propensity for trouble. When the bells do ring, I want to be able to say, "Alethos aneste," Risen Indeed, rather than dropping my saw and running (*ring-a-ding,* the bells, *clackety-clack,* the hooves, et cetera). Now is the time for all good kallikanzaroi . . . You know.

So . . .

Cassandra and I have this villa on the Magic Island. She likes it here. I like it here. She doesn't mind my indeterminate age anymore. Which is fine.

Just this early morning, as we lay on the beach watching the sun chase away stars, I turned to her and mentioned that this is going to be a big, big ulcer-giving job, full of headaches and such.

"No, it isn't," she replied.

"Don't minimize what is imminent," I said. "It makes for incompatibility."

"None of that either."

"You are too optimistic, Cassandra."

"No. I told you that you were heading into danger before, and you were, but you didn't believe me then. This time I feel that things should go well. That's all."

"Granting your accuracy in the past, I still feel you are underestimating that which lies before us."

She rose and stamped her foot.

"You *never* believe me!"

"Of course I do. It just happens that this time you're wrong, dear."

She swam away then, my mad mermaid, out into the dark waters. After a time she came swimming back.

"Okay," she said, smiling, shaking down gentle rains from her hair. "Sure."

I caught her ankle, pulled her down beside me and began tickling her.

"Stop that!"

"Hey, I believe you, Cassandra! Really! Hear that? Oh, how about that? I really believe you. Damn! You sure are right!"

"You are a smart-alecky kallikanz—Ouch!"

And she was lovely by the seaside, so I held her in the wet, till the day was all around us, feeling good.

Which is a nice place to end a story, *sic:*